MIND OF DISTINCTION

MIND OF DISTINCTION
HAWTHORN ACADEMY BOOK SEVEN

D.R. PERRY

DISRUPTIVE IMAGINATION

THE MIND OF DISTINCTION TEAM

Thanks to our JIT Readers

Rachel Beckford
Dave Hicks
Veronica Stephan-Miller

Editor
SkyHunter Editing Team

Version 1.00, August 2021
(Previously published as a part of the megabook *Hawthorn Academy: Year Three*)
ebook ISBN: 978-1-64971-996-6
Print ISBN: 978-1-64971-997-3

CHAPTER ONE

"This is creepier than I thought it would be."

"Peep!"

At least my dragonet agreed. The stairs down to the basement in the apartment in The Point were musty, damp, bare concrete.

"I wonder if they'll let us put a rug down here or something." Logan shrugged. "It echoes an awful lot. Hurts the ears don't you think?"

"I hoped it'd be a little, you know, homier." I sighed.

"I like it." Noah snorted. "Fits my new vampiness. Complements it, actually. Maybe even makes a fashion statement, like Dorian's wardrobe."

"Noah, honestly." Elanor held up her key ring, jangling the bobs of metal against each other. "Don't be so melodramatic. It's not like vampires are new. Or that you're the first one to get turned as a teenager either."

"Technically, I'm an adult." He held his hand out and gazed at his maroon-painted fingernails.

"I'm about to catch up to you." I chuckled.

"Nope." Noah shook his head. "Can't catch me; I'm the ginger fang man."

"Thought that was your boyfriend." Logan grinned. "Because Jonah's a redhead. Get it?"

After a moment absent of the laughter Logan expected, he slapped his hand over his mouth.

"No, no, I get it." Noah shrugged. "Or maybe I'm not getting any with Jonah in jail. Open the door already, El."

Elanor stuck the key in the lock and tried turning. Nothing happened.

"I just picked these up this morning." She blinked. "I don't understand."

"Peep!"

"Meow?"

"What is it, Doris?" Logan called after his mercat as she ran up the stairs.

The door at the top opened and briefly let in light. Thankfully artificial. It got blocked by the bulk of the person standing in the doorway.

"Trouble with the key?" The voice was a warm tenor, but gravelly somehow, as though the speaker had swallowed water down the wrong pipe a minute ago.

"Yeah, I'm afraid so, Mr. Micello." Elanor pushed past us, heading up the stairs to meet the man coming down it halfway.

He reached out, flipped a switch, and a bare bulb went on over her head. His face was broad and round, with a physique to match. He clung to both handrails as he descended, which I noticed were reinforced.

I narrowed my eyes, almost closing them, trying to get in touch with my sense of the magic around me. Something about Paolo Micello felt familiar, but I couldn't place from where. If he was an extrahuman of some sort, I wanted to know what kind.

He's a troll, of course. Like your friend. What's his name? Begins with a b and ends with an r. Oh, you know, from Gallows Hill.

"Bartholomew!"

"No, that's my nephew. But you've met him along with others I call kin." He nodded. "Which is one reason I agreed to rent this apartment in the first place."

"Oh." Elanor blinked and backed down the stairs.

"I'm sorry about the key. It goes to the apartment on the third floor, which is also for rent but unsuitable for a vampire. If you happen to know anyone else looking for a place," he glanced at Logan and me. "A nice young couple perhaps, please inform me."

He reached for a ring of keys on his belt and removed a set, then held them up while squinting. "My eyesight isn't what used to be. I mistook the B for three." He chuckled. "Let's switch, and you'll be all set."

"Thanks." Elanor exchanged keyrings with Mr. Micello.

"If you need help moving, that's Bartholomew's summer job. Let me know, and I'll send him over with the truck."

"That'd be super helpful," Noah said. "My hours are...limited, Mr. Micello."

"Understood. And call me Paolo."

He turned and headed back up the steps with a painfully stiff gait. Either Paolo Micello feared stairs or had trouble with his legs.

Why not both?

I narrowed my eyes and tried to visualize what my inside voice, which maybe wasn't so much evil as terrifyingly pragmatic, meant. Tiny flecks of reddish-gold dazzled me, collected somewhere around Paolo's knees. What that signified, I didn't know. Once the door closed behind him, Logan elbowed me.

"Write it down." He held my phone, which he'd managed to take out of my bag without my noticing. "Or type. And sorry about picking your pocket."

I glanced up, wondering whether Noah and Elanor had noticed this exchange. They were too busy opening the door. We followed them inside, me tapping out a memo on my phone about Paolo's spark-infested legs for later.

"Wow." Logan stopped so suddenly that I bumped into him.

"Whoa!"

We tumbled to the floor together, his arm caught in the strap on my bag. Ember swooped out of nowhere and caught my phone a hair before it fell on the floor. She landed while holding the electronic device against her scaly little face.

"Peep?"

Doris sauntered up to stand beside Ember, where she sat with her tail curled around her legs. The look she gave us reminded me of Professor Luciano, who died protecting us only a short span of weeks ago. I burst into tears, my awkward tangle with Logan suddenly transformed. I clung to him like a rock in the rapids.

Ember's eyes widened. She headbutted the mercat, knocking her off-center and breaking the impression. As though in apology, Doris ran to my side, rubbed against my shoulder, and purred.

"Hey." Logan touched my face and wiped away tears. "Hey, Aliyah. You're gonna be okay."

"He won't. Not ever again." I sniffled.

"Hawkins said this is normal." Tears stained his face too.

"I'm tired of feeling like this." I shuddered and leaned back. "Like any minute I'll go to pieces."

"Me too." Logan sat across from me now, our hands still clasped.

"I don't know what to do."

"Me neither."

Fabric rustled beside us.

"You're not alone." Noah's hand felt cool and soothing against my cheek.

"Yeah." Elanor hugged her brother. "That's why we rented this flop-house in the first place."

"You never gave us the ten-cent tour." I used my sleeve to dab under my eyes.

"As you can see, we've got this lovely linoleum, circa nineteen eighty-five."

"You doofus." Elanor rolled her eyes. "This design is clearly from the early nineties."

Just like that, we all laughed. For Logan and me, it was wet and snotty, with something sharp inside that still threatened. However, I was a fire magus and he was water. Both of us were accustomed to volatility, only not so emotional.

"Let's show them the bathroom first," Elanor said.

"Yeah. Don't want literally snot-nosed whippersnappers in my bedroom." Noah's attempted snort had a little too much sniffle in it. So he shared this grief also, but in a less obvious way.

The bathroom was right behind us. When Noah pushed the door inward, I expected a tiny room. Instead, it opened to my left into a decently sized space, decorated in Pepto-Bismol pink. The shower-head side of the bathtub sat behind it, the bar hanging bare without even rings for a curtain. A sizeable cabinet supported the sink, which stood between the tub/shower and toilet.

Logan stepped up to it and splashed his face several times. Then he turned, hands and face dripping. No towel hung from the ring by the sink or the hooks on the wall to my right.

"Oops." He blinked.

"Here." I reached into my bag and brought out a pack of tissues.

"Nah, this is better." Elanor held out a dishtowel.

"Oh." Logan reached for it but paused. "You were never this nice when I made mistakes back ho—I mean in Vegas."

"I don't have to pretend anymore." She shook the towel. "Go on."

He dried his face, then folded the towel and hung it neatly beside the sink. He gazed down at the damp pink porcelain, unmoving.

All those fine manners of his. Which of those were written in blood, do you think?

Angry red and orange lines in trails like the ones that come from staring at a light for too long crossed his back, superimposed over his clothes. I swallowed around a sudden lump in my throat.

"Let's call Bar." Elanor tugged her brother's sleeve. "And get out of here so Aliyah can wash up."

He nodded and scooted past me, not looking up, which was normal for Logan some of the time. But not for now. I could tell by the way his shoulders stood high like they reached for his ears.

"We're going to be okay." I squared my jaw and reached for the faucet. "All of us."

I felt Noah's presence in the doorway behind me although he didn't speak. Somehow, I sensed his abject disagreement. Instead of responding to that, I splashed my face thoroughly. Once the tight sting of tearstains eased, I closed the tap and made use of the towel.

"Let's finish that tour, then." Noah turned on his heel and led me out of the bathroom.

Elanor and Logan joined, having finished their call in the kitchen. There was plenty of room in there for a table and chairs. A set of wooden pocket doors slid aside to reveal a windowless living room. It had a bricked-over fireplace with a marble mantel. One of those faux flame lights squatted on the hearth. Noah sauntered over toward it, chuckling.

"This is what sold me on the place."

"Fun."

"It gets better." Elanor grinned. She headed for a door to the right of the fireplace, which I couldn't imagine led to anything bigger than a closet.

I was wrong.

It opened out into a room padded with thick noise-canceling tiles. A mic stand, an amp, a keyboard, and a stand holding an electric bass and an acoustic guitar filled most of the floor space.

"Welcome to Piercing Whispers central."

"Has Dylan seen this?" Logan asked.

"Later. He's still on shift at the Lyceum."

"So, where are your rooms?" I leaned against the mantel.

"Off that hall." Noah paced toward me, then linked his arm through mine. "Check it out."

Two doors led off the hallway, and each already had a sign on it, indicating whose room was whose. Noah's was a collage of construction paper decorated in rainbows. Elanor's sign was painted plywood decorated with FiFi's molted feathers.

"Luckily, the closets are the same size." She pushed her door open. The only thing in her room was a perch for her phoenix. "We'll be redecorating, obvs."

"Yeah." I nodded. "You got a great space here. How much did it run you?"

"Not much." Noah shrugged. "Some of it's barter. We're playing one free gig per month for Paolo. Did you know the Micellos own The Baybridge?"

"No, I didn't." I gave him a side-eye Izzy would have been proud of. "You're getting a job though, right?"

"Security." Noah nodded. "For the Ambersmiths, overnight."

"What about you?" Logan asked Elanor.

"Nothing yet. I applied all over town, though."

"Well, Paolo must think Piercing Whispers is something else." Logan picked at his thumbnail. "Renting to someone without a job. Or he's got some ulterior motive."

"You worry too much, Lo."

"Think I've earned the right."

I reached out, grabbed Logan's hand and squeezed, like he'd done for me the day after Professor Luciano died saving Noah and me. He glanced at me, eyes wide for a moment before nodding.

"Shouldn't someone be at Hawthorne Street when Bar gets there?" I asked.

"Yeah." Noah nodded. "Team kid siblings, you're on moving truck duty. El, we should check out that *bodega* across the street, see what they've got. I'm borderline hangry."

"Mood." Elanor patted her stomach. "There's nothing in the fridge."

We said goodbye at the door on the side of the house, where the basement stairs let out. For a moment, I watched them crossing Palmer Street toward Tropica Mart. Then, I turned and headed up the sidewalk with Logan.

"Should we text Cadence?" he asked. "Doesn't she live near here?"

"Yeah, she does. But she said something about going to Boston today."

"Oh." We walked all the way up Lafayette in silence. "Hey, look!" He pointed at the window for Engine House.

Brianna stood at the register inside.

"That's some good news." I sighed.

"Yeah. After getting laid off from Walgreen's, she was so worried. Should we go in and say hi?"

"I don't think there's time. The line in there is huge."

We caught her eye and waved enthusiastically before turning to walk up Derby Street toward Hawthorne.

Bar's truck was already in the driveway, and he stood shuffling his feet on the stoop outside as though he wasn't sure which bell to ring.

"Hey, Bar."

He turned, raising his eyebrows. "Oh. Hey, Aliyah. Logan."

"It's the one on the right." I reached into my bag and got my keys. "But no need to ring."

"How much stuff do they got?"

"Suitcases, a table and chairs, a futon." I opened the door and let the guys through. "That's all I'm sure about. My folks were in the basement when I left. Who knows what else they unearthed?"

In the living room at the top of the stairs, we found all the luggage and boxes. Bar hefted the entire stack of boxes with a suitcase balanced on top and carried them down the stairs without even pausing to catch his breath. Logan and I dragged the rest of the cases plus Noah's old knapsack, which he'd filled with adult coloring books and colored pencils.

Mom and Dad stood beside the truck, trying to offer Bar help putting everything in the back. He didn't need it. By the time Logan and I set the luggage down, the boxes were safely stowed.

"We've got furniture out back," Dad said.

"Kitchen stuff and some linens too," Mom added.

We made something like an assembly line, passing bags and boxes along the path that Bar navigated with the futon, table, chairs, and a pair of bed frames that looked like they could be bunked if desired.

"What about mattresses?" I shook my head. "Those frames aren't any good without them."

"That was my housewarming gift." Bubbe emerged from her office carrying a pair of handled grocery bags, sides bulging. "Ordered them yesterday. They're arriving on Palmer Street in about an hour."

"What are those for, then?" Logan stared at the bags, which smelled heavenly.

"Everyone helping out, of course." Bubbe grinned. "Rugelach and three kinds of babka. And a treat for Noah along with the recipe."

"'Scuse me for asking but is he gonna be able to eat at all?" Bar cleared his throat. "On account of being, well, a vampire."

"A dear friend recommended it." Bubbe nodded. "There are very few things vampires can eat, but she's got nearly two centuries of experience sampling them."

"Doctor Elizabeth!" I smiled. "How's she doing?"

"Well. She'll be up for the masquerade ball in October and staying with me."

"Cool." Logan elbowed me. "Third-years are allowed to go to that."

"We'd better tell Grace, then. And make sure you've got extra shoes."

"Not so fast, you two." Mom shook her head. "They haven't selected a new headmaster yet. The rules might change."

"Bummer." Bar sighed. "I hope you all can go. Our whole class from Gallows Hill will be there. Anyway, is there anything else going in the truck? There's still room."

"That's all." Dad nodded. "Thanks, Bartholomew."

"Hey!"

Everyone turned to see who had called down the driveway. A figure ran up it in the dark. As it drew nearer, I recognized Dylan Khan.

"Dylan!" Logan darted out to meet him, and they hugged.

"Is this all going to Noah's new place?"

"Yeah."

"Can I go with?"

"They're expecting you." I nodded.

"Cool." He smiled. "I've got news too. Mom's coming to work at Hawthorn."

"Whoa!" Logan clapped his hands. "Awesome! What's she doing?"

"School counselor." Dylan shrugged, clearly less excited than his roommate. "Trustees don't want Hawkins doing that while teaching full time."

"Oh." I blinked. "Hmm."

"What's wrong?" Logan stopped bouncing and glanced at Dylan.

"Could get awkward." Dylan sighed. "Like, if I ever happen to need help or whatever."

"Well, my door's always open." Bubbe handed me two bags of food, then set the third one in the cab of the truck with Bar.

"Wow, thanks." The corners of Dylan's mouth turned up.

"Now, you kids ought to get going if Elanor and Noah want to get those bed frames set up before the mattresses arrive." Bubbe went back up the steps in front of her office.

"Yes, and remember that Aliyah and Logan still have curfews to meet."

"Right, eleven-thirty." Logan nodded. "Which gives us two hours."

"Thanks, Morgensterns!" Bar waved out the window. "See half of you back on Palmer Street."

After he pulled away, Logan, Dylan, and I headed back toward The Point on foot.

I sat with Noah in his room and tried to put the bed frame together, which would only have been more frustrating if it had come from IKEA.

"Gimme the monkey wrench."

I slapped a length of metal into his waiting hand.

"No, wait. The Allen wrench."

I replaced it.

"Almost done?" I peered apprehensively at the contraption sagging around him.

Noah threw his head back and let out a laugh that almost sounded like a howl.

"Need help?" Logan stood in the doorway.

"Go help El." Noah waved him away.

"We're done with hers."

"Then have at it, gadget man." Noah stood and stepped out of the rickety-looking excuse for a bed frame.

"That's not bad. Like, for a parody." Dylan strummed the acoustic guitar in the corner and sang. "Gadget man, fixing up his furniture alone. And it isn't gonna take a long, long time. To get this bed set up in here. I'm not the man that's gonna sleep in it, but the one who does is gonna sleep alone. But Noah, he's not a gadget man. Gadget man, top of the class at the place I call home."

"That's pretty good, Dyl." Noah grinned. "Figure out how to make it less derivative, and we've got a new number, I think."

"You really want him writing songs about you sleeping alone?" Elanor chuckled.

"No. But at least he's honest." Noah sighed.

"Got it." Logan stood while dropping the slide wrench into the tool bucket. "Just in time, too."

A truck horn sounded outside.

We all got out of the way as the delivery staff brought in two mattresses and box springs. They left in a hurry, making me think at least one of them was a little weirded out by being in an apartment designed for vampires. We unwrapped the plastic and set the beds on the frames ourselves with little trouble.

"How was that Tropica Mart?" I opened the fridge, looking for drinks to go with the babka, but only saw bottled blood. "Nothing much there besides this?"

"Not true." Elanor shook her head. "I drank all the pineapple Faygo."

"Cadence swears by that stuff." I chuckled. "Is it still open?"

"All night. It's a twenty-four-hour sort of place," Noah answered.

"Come on." Dylan leaned the guitar against the wall and headed for the door with us.

"Are you guys coming?" I glanced back at Logan and Elanor.

"Nah." He shook his head. "Can you get me some ginger ale if they have it?"

"Sure."

The Tropica Mart had a sign out front with the picture of a palm tree underneath a crescent moon. The brown-skinned man sitting under it exhibited a fangy smile. I understood why Noah was so enthused to go back to the clearly vamp-friendly establishment.

Inside, the shelves were close together and packed with a variety of grocery and household goods. A fresh fruit and vegetable stand sat at the back, near coolers filled with frosty beverages. I saw plantains, coconuts, papaya, jicama, yucca, tomatillos, and avocados along with apples, oranges, and pears.

"Oh, is this your *hermana?*"

"Yeah, it is." Noah nodded at the man behind the counter, who might have modeled for the figure on the sign. "Jefe, this is my sister Aliyah. Aliyah, Jefe."

"Jefe DelSangre. This is my store." He held his hand out, and I shook it. "Welcome."

"Thank you." I smiled. "Nice to meet you."

We gathered soda, which was mostly the Faygo brand. They had all the flavors, including ginger ale. After paying and wishing Jefe a good evening, we headed back across the street. At the apartment, we drank soda while unpacking linens and making beds. Logan and I had to go after that, but Dylan stuck around to get the drums set up in the practice room.

"Who's going to play them?" I asked. "Arick went back to Bergen."

"His parents own an airline. So he's coming and going a lot this summer."

"How's that going to work for your monthly gigs at the Baybridge?" Logan blinked.

"Maybe you'll fill in if he's not around?" Elanor shuffled her feet. "I meant to ask more nicely than that."

"No." He planted his feet. "No performing. Not anymore."

"Okay." She nodded. "I understand."

She doesn't.

The voice was right, but I wasn't going to start an argument and miss curfew.

"I'll ask Azrael tomorrow. His dad knows most of the musicians in this town." I shrugged. "For now, we've got to get home."

We left. Out on Lafayette Street, Logan spoke.

"Thanks."

"What did I do?"

"You backed me up." He turned, walking backward like Dorian did last year before Mercy died. In true Logan Pierce fashion, he looked at my face without meeting my gaze. "She would have kept asking if you hadn't mentioned Az. Eventually, I would have been their drummer. Whether I liked it or not."

"Hey, this is what friends do for each other."

"No. Dylan didn't say anything, and he's my friend. We're close." He cleared his throat. "But you're my best friend, Aliyah. Ever."

We stopped to hug on the corner of Lafayette and Derby, then held hands the rest of the way home. He walked me up the stoop in front of my parent's apartment.

"See you tomorrow morning for waffles?" He grinned.

"Yeah. I promise not to try passing ketchup off as syrup. Goodnight, Logan."

"Goodnight, Aliyah."

I ran up the front stairs as fast as I could, peered out the window, and was rewarded for my effort as I watched Logan walk through the door at Bubbe's office, Doris pacing in beside him.

"Peep." Ember nuzzled my cheek, cooing. Then she yawned.

"Yeah, girl. Let's get some sleep."

I only paused by Mom's office to wave at her before heading to my room for pajamas, the toothbrush, and bed.

C H A P T E R   T W O

The week before I turned eighteen, I stood in the kitchen.

"Mom, I have to take the extramagus test." I crossed my arms over my chest. "What are we doing about that?"

"Bubbe's still hammering out the details with the Director-General." She poured coffee. "There are still five days before your birthday."

"She's not still trying to get me out of it?" I tapped my foot. "You know how I feel about that."

"I know." Mom toppled a splash of cream into her cup. "And yes, she is trying to make the process easier."

"How does that work, exactly? If I'm an adult, she doesn't get to make that kind of decision for me."

"Which is why she's making arrangements now, while you're still a minor." Mom clinked a spoon in the clouded coffee and stirred.

"You know, Aliyah," Dad interrupted. "It has to happen after you turn eighteen, but there's no requirement for you to have it on your birthday."

"I didn't ask you, Dad." My arms dropped to my sides as the implications of what he said hit me. "Oh. Oh!"

"Aaron!" The air around my mother got warmer.

"I want things to be fair, Angie." Dad sighed. "For Aliyah and everyone else."

"That's why Bubbe's having those talks, so it'll be different this time." Mom said.

"Different only for me?" I narrowed my eyes. "It needs to change for every extramagus. Or else none of us. If Bubbe's planning to get me some special waiver, I'm going to say no."

"I don't want anyone else tortured either." Mom held her coffee in front of her like a shield. "Bubbe thinks you shouldn't have to put yourself through the full ordeal. She's using the summer to your advantage."

"What do you mean?"

"Available space and facilities give her an excuse to request a truncated process." Mom sighed. "Your recent acts of heroism are under consideration, too."

"Hawthorn had all the space and facility they needed for Dylan." I leaned against the counter. "And me."

"There's still no headmaster at Hawthorn. So until the trustees select and appoint one, the test can't happen on campus."

"Do I still get a witness?" I raised an eyebrow.

"That depends."

"That's bullshit." I glared, nostrils flaring, practically daring her to jump on my case for language. Instead, she sighed.

"You can postpone the test until proper facilities are available, but you've got to put it in writing and hand it directly to the Director-General. In person."

"Great. Where is he?"

"Bubbe mentioned the Hawthorne Hotel," Dad offered. "I'd wait until after the dinner hour to see him, though."

"Aliyah—"

"You can't talk me out of this, Mom."

"I know." She pushed the door to her office open. "You can use the guest account on my computer to write your request. I'll print it while you're out. Hold on."

Mom sat at her desk and switched accounts to the one Noah and I used on occasion.

"Thanks."

It took a few moments to compose my thoughts. Then I wrote something more formal than I might have managed without that pause.

Fix it. You don't want to sound...unhinged.

"Never turn in the first draft."

"Hmm?" Dad said from the kitchen.

"Something Logan says at school."

I finished after a few more minutes of work, but something was missing. I stood and paced while trying to remember how letters Mom sent to schools always looked.

"It needs addresses," Mom said. "I'll fix it. You were due down at Bubbe's to help out."

"Right." I nodded. "Thanks, Mom."

She sat at the desk and nodded without looking up. I left, heading out in the kitchen to let her work. More frustration must have shown on my face than I'd intended.

"Hey, Aliyah." Dad put his hand on my shoulder. "You know she's only trying to protect you, right?"

"I know, but she's not an extramagus. I have to do this my way or not at all."

"I get it. I'm proud of you for standing up. But you have to jump through the hoops first. You understand?"

"Yeah, Dad. I do. Thanks for reminding me of that."

I headed down the back stairs, and knocked at the bottom instead of barging in.

"Come in!"

I walked into Bubbe's office and closed the door. Ember swooped through the air above my head, flying up and down the hall. She peered into each room at the boarders and critters there for checkups. I went straight to the small kitchen in the middle of the hall, turning the corner to find Logan sitting over a bunch of patient files and paperwork. My grandmother bustled at the stove, boiling water.

"What's that there?" I peered over Logan's shoulder.

"They're about Doris." Logan tapped one of the papers. "We're trying to figure out what type of mercat she is. These are genetic tests."

"That's advanced work. Must be exciting for you." I sat beside him.

"Exciting for Doris too." He grinned. "She wants to know where she came from."

"Meow." Doris jumped up on the table and paced back and forth. She peered at the files, then bumped her head against my hand while purring.

"I guess that means she's doesn't mind me seeing them." I smiled.

"Yeah. Doris really likes you. I mean, you did save her life."

"That's not how I remember it."

"You carried her down the street to here."

"Oh, yeah. I barely remember that. But you gave her water."

"That's the part I forget." He chuckled.

"I'm bringing this decoction to the opossum in room two," Bubbe said. "I'll be back in about five minutes."

"Okay." Logan nodded.

I waited until I heard Bubbe crooning in the treatment room.

"I need your help." I drew a deep breath before letting the hard part out. "They're making me take an extramagus test. I want you to be my witness."

"What?" Logan blinked. "Extramagus test?" His voice cracked.

"Anyone with more than one element has to. I wasn't allowed to tell anybody, but I guess I'm telling you they exist because otherwise, I can't ask you to be there with me."

"They test every extramagus? But why? And how?"

"I'll tell you another time." I glanced at the open door. "It's a secret."

"It must be horrible if it's unspoken." He picked at the ragged skin by his thumbnail, a habit when something disturbed him.

"I found out when Dylan went through it last year. He chose me."

"Okay, then."

"Are you sure? You can change your mi—"

"It's utterly horrible?"

"Terrifying. Been dreading it all year."

"You don't need to tell me more. I'll be there, no matter what. Like I promised."

Doris jumped into my lap, purring. Ember landed on my shoulder, gazed down at the mercat, *peeped* once, then hopped on Logan's shoulder where she curled herself around his neck in a familiar fashion.

"She hasn't done that in a long time." Logan nodded at Doris.

I glanced at Ember. "Likewise." I rested my chin on one hand while petting Doris with the other. "So what's this about a genetics test?"

Logan launched into a lecture about chromosomes, alleles, and genetic markers commonly found in mercats. His enthusiasm for the subject made it more interesting than it would've been if I'd read it or even if Bubbe had explained it.

I spent the rest of the day in the extraveterinary office with Logan after going over the file. We fed and watered the boarded animals and took some to the backyard for exercise. After that, it was time for lunch.

We headed down the driveway. Izzy sat on her porch with Lee. After a brief conversation, they both joined us at Engine House for pizza.

It's hard enough to keep secrets from a clairvoyant. When Cadence the gossipy mermaid plopped down beside us, my privacy was a lost cause.

"Aliyah, you look off." Cadence peered at my face. "Iz, pull a card for her."

Izzy reached for the bag with her cards.

"Don't." I shook my head. "I've got kind of a big ask. Just Cadence and Izzy, but I trust you to keep this on the down-low, Lee." I picked a bit of cheese off the crust on my plate.

Izzy narrowed her eyes. "I don't like this, Aliyah."

"It's worse than that." Logan patted my shoulder.

"Oh?" Cadence raised her eyebrow while glancing from Logan to me.

"I'm serious. This is some 'never again' level stuff. Are you sure you want to hear it? Because I can't unsay any of this."

"Go on." Cadence leaned forward, elbows on the table.

"Spill it," Izzy ordered.

Lee nodded.

"After I turn eighteen, I've got to take a test because I'm an extramagus. I saw one happen last year, to Dylan. It's absolutely inhumane, like being tortured with every kind of elemental magic that exists. If enough people knew, maybe they'd find another way. So I want to record mine and leak it to the public, but I need your help."

Logan covered my hand with his. Cadence's eyes widened. Izzy nodded, and chewed on the inside of her cheek. Lee leaned back in his chair, lips pressed into a thin, flat line. He surprised me by speaking first.

"That's why he was off all last year." It wasn't a question but a statement of fact.

"I wish he'd said something." Cadence sighed. "Everyone assumed all his drama came from breaking up with Grace."

"He wasn't allowed to talk about it." I narrowed my eyes, trying to keep tears out of them. "I get one witness who has to be a magus. I chose Logan. The rest of you aren't supposed to know this. Or even be there when it happens."

Izzy's thrummed her fingers against the table. "So, how do we help?"

"With press coverage, of course." Cadence smirked. "At least that's my best guess. If you want to blow this thing wide open, my mom can make it happen."

"You've got it, Cadence."

"What's the other part?" Izzy tugged at the strap on the satchel she carried her cards in. "All I've got to offer is my skill with my cards."

"No. Like it or not, you're the most popular girl at Messing, Izzy. You've got connections. What I need is some way to pull the entire experience out of my head and share it. Are there psychics who can do anything like that?"

"Usually, that's a telepath." Izzy shook her head. "I don't know any, but Jacinda might be able to help you."

"She's Messing's cheer squad captain." Logan nodded. "A memory psychic, right?"

"Exactly." Izzy nodded. "If there's something you need to make sure somebody sees, a memory psychic is what you want. They can put your memory into an item, and anyone who activates it will see what happened from your point of view."

"Wow. Do you think she'd help us, though?"

"No idea," Izzy said. "She's kind of an introvert."

"She mentioned that Bar's her cousin." Logan traced shapes in the condensation on his soda cup. "Maybe he can help."

"I don't want him involved." I shook my head.

"Why? Because it's dangerous?" Cadence grinned. "Bar's a big boy, with powers to match."

I opened my mouth, about to say exactly what I thought.

Don't tell her it's because he's still hung up on her.

"Last year, danger got my professor killed." I made a fist and crushed the paper plate in the middle of it, pizza crust and all.

"You act like a sponge, not a mermaid." Izzy glanced at a card in her hand. She put it away without showing us. "You soak up every bad attitude your edgelord boyfriend puts on."

"Are you sure Crow's her boyfriend? Because that's subject to change." Logan's catty question made my mouth drop open.

"Why, Mr. Pierce. I never would've dreamed you had it in you." Cadence shrugged. "It's complicated. He's on thin ice."

"Good." Logan put his palms flat on the table, actually looking her in the eye. "I'm sick of people getting hurt. I'm not letting it happen this year."

"I'd love to chat with you about calculated risk." Cadence nodded, her auburn curls bobbing. "This isn't about one evil person. One of our best friends is facing off against persecution. The danger here isn't my fault, or Crow's." She raised an eyebrow at me. "Right, Aliyah?"

"I don't know." I sighed. "Both of you are right, but we should be more careful, not less."

Silence stretched. Eventually, I felt a presence nearby. I looked up to find Brianna Collins holding a pitcher of soda.

"Sorry. I guess I walked in on something?"

"Just talking about last year."

"Are you all okay?"

"Yeah," Logan answered.

"Thanks for the soda," Cadence said.

Brianna looked like she was about to say more when the bell above the door jingled. Elanor sauntered in with Noah, Dylan, and someone I didn't expect to see today.

"Is that Arick Magnuson?" Lee blinked. "From Norway?"

"His parents own an airline," Logan said.

The bandmates sat at the next table and leaned across to chat after giving their order to Brianna. Nobody mentioned the extramagus test. But the conversation about the future didn't stop there.

"So I hear your mom's the new counselor," Lee said. "It's going to be cool, finally meeting Dylan's parents."

"Parent. No Dad, just Mom."

"Why?" Cadence blinked.

"They split up."

"That's pretty heavy," Logan said. "Are you okay?"

"I guess." Dylan shrugged, worrying the napkin with his fingers. "They started arguing last fall. Think I've got something to do with it."

There's an elephant in this room.

I walked up and punched it in the trunk.

"Because you're an extramagus?"

"Probably. Mom filed divorce papers before I came out to them." Dylan sighed.

"I bet it's not about you." Noah patted his shoulder.

"Either way, it sucks." Izzy shook her head. "Let me know if you want a reading."

"Some other time." Dylan waved a hand. "We've got all summer."

"Are you sure you're okay?" I asked.

"Mom told me last month. Besides, I talked about it already." He glanced at Noah, then Elanor. "Bandmates are mates."

"Right." Noah elbowed him.

"Speaking of mates." Cadence glanced at Noah. "Have you seen Jonah?"

"They're only letting family visit. I've sent letters. He hasn't written back. I don't know why."

"Maybe he can't send anything out. Or his lawyer advised against it," Elanor said. "You'll talk sooner or later."

"I don't know." Izzy's brow furrowed. "Hang on." She pulled out a card. "Crap on a crap cracker."

"Share with the class?" Dylan said.

"It ain't nothing nice." Izzy slapped the card on the table.

It was The Chariot reversed, which meant something wrong with communication, usually deliberate.

"Let's hope any ban on letters out is prison-wide," Logan said. "Nobody wants Temperance sending out manifestos while she's locked up."

"She's not in the same place." Noah shook his head. "They put her in some white-collar juvie hall down in New York. It's totally unfair."

"But she's a murderer." Logan blinked.

"Her parents are saying she was duped, led down a dark path." Noah snorted. "By Alex Onassis."

"Weren't you calling him the prince of darkness last year?" Cadence raised an eyebrow.

"I can't stand the guy." Noah shook his head. "But Aliyah and I wouldn't be sitting here if he hadn't done the right thing at the last minute."

"Are you sure?" Izzy asked. "Because he definitely bought into all that magisupremacy."

"Temperance was worse." Arick snorted. "She handed out honest-to-gods fascist pamphlets. And blaming it on Alex? The guy who showed up bruised after their alone time?"

"I noticed." I shook my head. "Anyway, Coach Ives was her real boyfriend."

"What?" Cadence's mouth dropped open.

"The two of them were, um, intimate." I grimaced.

"Where did you hear that?" Izzy blinked.

"I overheard Mom," I answered. "He resigned when they got caught, and the state revoked his teaching license."

"I believe it." Arick nodded. "Nazis suck."

"Spoken like a true punk." Noah chuckled. "I mean that in the nicest possible way of course."

"Thanks." Arick grinned.

"Has she had her trial?" Logan asked.

"No." Noah shook his head. "There's a hearing, something about whether Jonah's coerced turning case is part of her murder charges. Her family's contesting his plea."

Elanor blew a raspberry. I nodded.

"When?" Logan pulled a pencil stub and a small notebook from his pocket.

"July," Noah answered. "I'm giving a statement. I'd appreciate some moral support."

"Can I give one, too?" I asked.

"I'm not sure, Aliyah." Noah shook his head. "You can offer, but they might not accept it because you're an extramagus."

I sighed. "Do they have that horrible device at least?"

"Yes. And the autopsy reports." Noah sipped his soda. "But it's a hearing, remember? They still have to decide whether me getting turned has anything to do with all that."

"If only Lotan could talk." Elanor glanced at the serpent sleeping on Noah's shoulder. "But what can you do?"

"Translate." Logan chuckled. "You know I can understand what they say, right?"

"No. I did not know that." Noah blinked.

"How long have you been able to do that?" Elanor narrowed her eyes at her brother.

"In my first year. Thought it was only Doris at first. But I under-stand all of them." He stared at his hands, his right one twitching as he tried to refrain from pulling a scab off his left thumb.

"Of course he kept it secret." I came to his rescue. "If your parents knew, what would they have done?"

"Had him committed." She paled. "That's the plan if he sets foot in Nevada ever again. They would've done it last summer if they'd known. Saw some nasty paperwork over winter break and that's why I moved out."

"Yeah." Logan stared at his uneaten pizza. "I figured. Feels like we're in a Grimm story. The kind where the parents end up eating their kids."

"What if they come to Parent's Night?" Elanor shuddered.

I looked around the table at all the wide-eyed faces. Dylan broke the silence.

"If they try anything funny, I'll conjure a tornado and drop a house on them."

Everybody chuckled a little, but nobody outright laughed. This humor was drier than a desert and twice as harsh. But as long as my friends could keep laughing, we could get through anything. Right?

That night, I leaned against the fence between the driveway and my backyard, gathering the courage to cross the street and head into the Hawthorne Hotel with my postponement letter. Could I face the Director-General? Would he accept my request if I stood there, visibly shaking? After watching him test Dylan, I feared him.

It's worse. The man terrifies you, with good reason.

Because I was alone, I answered my inside voice, which wasn't acting particularly evil.

"Thanks for understanding. But I don't know what to do."

Hand him the letter at your grandmother's appointment, perhaps?

"I don't want to risk her stopping me."

So go. Quake in your sandals if you must. You're not alone.

"That's right." I nodded at Ember, who sat on my left shoulder. "You'll help me be brave, right girl?"

"Brave for what?"

Don't be alarmed.

I turned slowly. The voice was right because Logan stood peering over the fence from the backyard.

"I didn't know you were out here."

"Likewise. What's going on?"

I told him.

"I'll go with you if you want."

"I do. But you're busy."

He jerked a thumb over his shoulder. "It's time for the opossums to go back inside, anyway."

"I'll help."

I strode through the gate Logan held open. The simple yet challenging task of wrangling baby opossums onto their mother's back and escorting them back to their room lifted my spirits. Maybe it was Logan's enthusiasm. Or both.

Absolutely both.

"Yeah."

Logan noticed my gaffe but said nothing. Did he not care about my habit of replying to nobody? Or did he think I communicated with Ember the way he did with Doris? At least he didn't seem to judge me for it.

Sooner or later you have to tell somebody about me.

I ignored the voice this time.

"Where are you headed?" Logan walked beside me down the driveway.

"I've got to hand a letter to an, um, intimidating person."

"This is about that test." Logan sighed. "How can I help?"

"Do you remember the first Parents Night dance?"

"Yeah. We hid your solar. But he knows you're an extramagus."

"It's not magic I need to hide, Logan." I sighed. "It's fear."

"Oh." He blinked. "Maybe you want someone braver than me."

"You've got plenty of courage."

"He's in the hotel?" Logan changed the subject.

"Yeah. Mom put the room number right on the letter."

"Let's cross the street then."

"Meow." Doris walked ahead of us, like a standard-bearer.

The front door at the Hawthorne Hotel was still open after dinner, the likeliest time for Director-General Rockport to be in his room. We turned left toward the bank of elevators. My finger trembled over the up button, but I managed to press it. The elevator opened immediately. Inside, my hands shook too much to select the floor.

Logan stilled the paper flapping in my grasp and glanced at the address on top. I let him take it from me. When he selected the fourth floor, the elevator closed its doors.

The pit of my stomach would've sunk anyway, but the elevator felt like it sent my guts straight to hell. That's an atypical thought for a Jewish girl like me, but that entire evening felt less normal by the minute. When the elevator opened, the hallway yawned in front of me like a gullet, the red paisley carpet and maroon striped wallpaper enhancing that impression.

Logan took my hand and led me down, glancing at the room numbers as we went. I followed, unable to do much more than measure my steps to match his pace. Doris brought up the rear this time.

"Peep." Ember nuzzled my cheek and wrapped her tail over my shoulder like a hug.

We stopped in front of his room. I didn't notice much about the door except that the knob was free and clear of the Do Not Disturb sign. At least I wouldn't feel like I was imposing.

"Hold this." Logan handed me the paper, the entire reason for my visit. "If you need, I'll do the talking. Formal introductions are like dancing for me."

He knocked solidly, four times. Muffled footsteps sounded on the other side. The door opened inward, revealing the man who'd haunted my nightmares since last autumn. He probably figured more frequently in Dylan's than mine now.

"Good evening, Director-General Rockport." Logan inclined his head in a gesture of respect. "Miss Aliyah Morgenstern is here to deliver a document concerning an appointment later this week."

Logan didn't look in the Director-General's eyes, but Rockport seemed to take Logan's mannerisms in stride.

He knows all the trustees, including Logan's father.

I almost replied to the voice. Instead, I addressed Director-General Rockport.

"I'm requesting a postponement of my test to a date and time when proper facilities and equipment are available at Hawthorn Academy." I held the letter out to him. "All the details are in the body of the letter, sir."

Good show, calling him sir.

"This is against the wishes of your grandmother." He raised an eyebrow as he perused the paper. "Nevertheless, as you must be an adult at the time of testing, it's not her decision. As unconventional as your choice may be, I'm inclined to honor it."

"Thank you, sir. I—"

"Conditionally. Give me a reason to postpone. The letter does not specify one." He looked me in the eye, no allowance for avoidance given the way he done with Logan.

"My experience should be fair. My knowledge of the process makes me think a modified test isn't equitable."

"Your knowledge?"

"I was the peer witness for Dylan Khan."

"Interesting." He tilted his head. "You will receive notice of your rescheduled date in August. Good evening."

He took one step back and closed the door. That's when my knees gave out.

"Whoa, Aliyah." Logan hooked his arm under mine, supporting my weight on one side as Ember flapped her wings on the other. Doris squeaked a few times.

"Right, Doris." Logan nodded. "Time to go."

He helped me down the hall and out of the Hawthorne Hotel. I'd carry the burden of the test all summer. I hadn't realized that before, but it wouldn't have stopped me anyway.

I stood on the back porch in the mist at six the next morning, peering through the haze at Ember flying from branch to branch in the mulberry tree. The door opened behind me. My grandmother leaned against the railing on my left, mug of tea in one hand, hair red as an autumn maple. The other held a postcard, which she slapped down on the railing between us.

"This arrived late last night. Read it."

"Your appointment has been postponed until further notice, per written request of one Aliyah Sarah Morgenstern. Director-General Walter Rockport, BEA."

"Aliyah, what have you done?"

"The right thing, Bubbe." I turned my head and met her gaze.

"I hope so."

"You know how I feel."

"Yes." She sighed and bowed her head. "You're not the only one with big emotions here. The first step on this path is the only easy one."

"The second one's the hardest." I put my hand over hers. "I know."

"You don't. That's what scares me, Bissel." She looked back up at me, eyes rimmed with red.

"Why do you keep acting like I didn't think this through, Bubbe?"

"Because that's impossible. You don't have enough information."

"So why didn't you give it to me?"

"I don't have it. Nobody possibly could." Her hands curled around warm ceramic. "Not even your mother, with all of her theory work."

"What about Logan?"

"Maybe he could have figured it out. Given more training than Hawthorn offers."

"Well, he helped me. Last night, delivering the letter. I was too scared to do it alone." I blinked, eyes suddenly damp. I glanced up, but despite the misty morning, it wasn't drizzling.

"At least that level of fear matches the danger." She shook her head. "I only wanted to spare you pain. Because I love you."

"I know, Bubbe. I love you too." I sniffled. "I care how you feel, so much. But since Dylan's test, I think about every other extramagus that doesn't have someone like you on their side."

"You're only eighteen. You can't save the world, Aliyah."

"I'm not trying to." I shook my head. "I want to spare them pain."

"It's unclear how your suffering will accomplish that." She set the tea down on the railing, covering the postcard. "But it's too late for me to change that now."

"I've got a plan. And help."

She opened her arms, and we hugged.

"All the same, I can't stop worrying."

"Why?"

"There's an old saying that when you have children, part of your heart lives outside your chest."

"That's harsh."

"Yes. And it doesn't soften for grandchildren."

"I'll be as careful as I can be, Bubbe. Because I love you."

She let go.

"And I you, Bissel. Forever and always."

CHAPTER THREE

In July, I stood in the exam room beside Logan, watching Bubbe remove a thorn from a moon hare's flank. It wasn't Grace's familiar Lune, thank goodness. Azrael's father found the poor critter under the bandstand on Salem Common.

"Once everything's sterilized, we must take extreme care," Bubbe explained. "If we touch anything but this shaved area, we'll need another tweezer."

"It's okay. She's helping." I tried comforting the poor hare, but she didn't seem particularly soothed by my words.

Logan stepped to my left, made eye contact with the frightened creature, and wiggled his nose. We saw the effects instantly. The hare lay back and extended her leg toward my grandmother. She took it in her gloved hand and brandished the tweezer over the puncture. The animal looked away from my grandmother but sat like a stone.

"Brave girl." Bubbe stepped away and tossed the thorn in the trash. "Now we'll patch it up."

The hare didn't need stitches, just a butterfly closure. Once Bubbe did that, she discarded her gloves and washed her hands. I brought the tray of soiled instruments to the sterilizer while Logan gathered the hare in his arms, humming as he carried her to a recovery room. He set her down, wiggled his nose a few more times, then let her rest on a cushion. He closed the Dutch door's bottom and joined me by the sterilizer.

His care for animals was miraculous as if he was born to help them. He had no ego at all about it, either. The longer I knew Logan, the more amazing I thought he was.

Tell him then.

The last time my inside voice encouraged me to express feelings like that, it went wrong. The moment passed, as they always had before.

"I would've had a much harder time without you Logan," Bubbe said behind us. "I hope you intend to visit frequently during the school year."

"Maybe I'll be in town." Logan sighed. "If I don't manage to get a scholarship, I'll ask to stay with Elanor. Maybe I can get a GED at the community college."

"Scholarship letters come in July. Have you checked with Mom?" I asked.

"Guess I spaced on the date." Logan shrugged. "I'll talk to her when we've finished."

"Okay." I closed the sanitizer and set the dial, then we washed our hands and headed upstairs.

It was about time for a snack anyway. Bubbe hadn't baked anything that day, and all the treats were upstairs until she went shopping that evening. I opened the cabinet for chips and salsa. Logan knocked on my mother's office. She emerged, closing the door behind her.

"How can I help you?"

"I wondered if my scholarship letter came in from Hawthorn." Logan lifted his hand and scratched the back of his head. "I don't want to be a pain, but my entire next year kind of depends on it."

"Hold on." Mom stepped back into her office.

I glimpsed someone inside but couldn't tell who. My father laughed in the living room at something on television.

"Who's in there?" I asked.

Doris chirped.

"Grace," Logan answered. "What if it's bad news?"

"Oh." I drew a deep breath. "I bet—"

"No, it's okay. You don't have to comfort me ahead of time." He pressed his lips together. "I'll be eighteen next month."

"Can't help it. I care."

He blinked and opened his mouth.

The door opened, and Mom emerged with Grace at her side. My mother raised an eyebrow at the chips. Grace gave them a longing look.

"Snacks for everyone." I grabbed the bag and poured more into the bowl, then pushed it toward them.

Everyone munched chips except for Logan, who rocked back and forth on his toes. When Mom noticed, she immediately brushed the crumbs off her hands.

"Logan and Grace have both received scholarships this year."

"How?" I blinked. "I thought they only gave one."

"What about Dylan?" Logan asked.

"Hawthorn didn't give any scholarships this year, just one work study. Dylan's mother works there now, so he gets tuition, room, and board as her family member."

"Mine's from Byers Beauty." Grace smiled. "I designed a makeup case and won my tuition. Ambersmith Fashions gave me a raise that more than covers my room and board."

"What about me?"

"A trustee's covering your third year."

"A trustee?" Logan blinked. "Not my father."

"No. Your benefactor is Hank Thurston. His offer is contingent, however. You must submit an early admissions application to Providence Paranormal College."

"No way." Logan's eyes widened. "That's my dream school."

"I'll give Mr. Thurston the good news." Mom smiled. "We'll work on your application over the rest of the summer."

"I never heard of a trustee handing out scholarships before." Grace shook her head. "And I've checked just about every scholarship opportunity in extrahuman society."

"Maybe the trustees aren't all like Mr. Fairbanks and—" I censored Logan's dad out of my musings. "And Mrs. Onassis."

"Oh, no." Logan glanced at me. "Sorry, Aliyah."

"Why?"

"PPC was your dream school too."

"I'm still applying." I grinned. "I think I'll make it."

"Oh, I almost forgot to tell you." Logan crunched chips. "Dorian has an app—"

The phone in Mom's office rang. She poked her head out and spoke. "Bubbe called. She says your friend's at her office."

We headed down the back stairs.

"Is it okay for me to be there?" Grace asked.

"Should be fine," I said.

We walked up the hall toward the lobby. Lune twitched his whiskers by the door where the stray moon hare slept but ultimately followed Grace. Dorian Spanos stood in the waiting room, signing in with Julia the strix on his shoulder. A married couple older than my parents sat behind him. She stared at nothing while he gazed at *Captivating Creatures Weekly* without touching it. I wondered if their unusual behavior came from their psychic abilities. They were only here because their magus son loved magical critters.

"Hey, Dorian." Logan waved.

"Hey yourself." He smiled, but less brightly than on the day we met last year.

"Come on back." Bubbe held the door.

Dorian followed her. We trailed behind him. I glanced over my shoulder to see his parents still sitting. Dorian's dad held the unopened magazine, his face wearing a bemused expression, as though reading an article without even flipping the cover over.

We went into the same exam room where Dylan bonded with Gale almost two years before. Bubbe opened the cabinet above the sink and pulled down a plastic container full of black and gold collars.

"Yeah." Dorian nodded. "We're formalizing a bond here. Plus the school paperwork stuff."

"Oh." Grace blinked. "It's okay that I'm here, right?"

"Sure. I'm glad you guys showed up. Mom and Dad mean well but don't get all this magus stuff."

"Does your dad do psychometry?"

"Yeah. He got a surprise the first time Julia said hello." Dorian grinned. "Said he always wanted to visit northern Italy, but in person, not through his hands."

"All right, let's see how Julia's doing." Bubbe bent her arm while smiling at the strix.

Julia hooted and hopped from Dorian's shoulder to Bubbe's forearm. She shook her feathers, then turned her head around before letting my grandma check her wings and examine her talons.

Julia had a sober personality, unlike Dorian's late familiar Mercy. She'd been ten pounds of mischief in a five-pound bag. The strix had always been stately and dignified. Since Professor Luciano died, she'd grown somber, too.

I watched Dorian sit through the examination, staring at everything and nothing at the same time. I didn't know how he felt. Losing a familiar was inevitable for most magi who bonded with them. Only a handful of magical creatures had comparable lifespans. Ember might even live longer than me.

Logan held Doris while studying Bubbe's examination process. Grace stood by the door, shifting her weight from one foot to the other as she stared down at Lune. Being unlikely to endure the same tragedy was no reason to neglect a friend in pain. I crossed the room and sat beside him.

"You okay?" I murmured.

"No." He sighed. "This is nothing nice."

"Can I help?"

"This does help." He closed his eyes and leaned against the wall. "Thanks."

Grace elbowed Logan, and they also sat by Dorian through the rest of Julia's physical. When he saw us there his shoulders eased slightly. We hadn't lifted his burden but maybe shared some of the weight.

"She's got a clean bill of health." Julia took off from her forearm and flew to Dorian's shoulder.

"Hello again, old bird." Dorian stroked her head, and she hooted.

"Are you both ready?" Bubbe held an unclasped black and gold bonding collar.

"Yeah." Dorian nodded. Logan peered at Julia, then nodded at Bubbe.

My grandmother handed the chain to Dorian. Purple, white, and gold lit around their hands. Bubbe had channeled her solar magic, and the ice came from Dorian. But what about the purple?

Julia, of course.

"Of course." I slapped my hand over my mouth.

"Inside voice," Grace murmured.

"Shh." Logan put a finger to his lips.

Dorian fastened the collar, and the magic surged again, this time without Bubbe's solar. The purple and white brought it all back like a blow to my chest, the same as that night in the locker room. Tears drenched my face.

You're not alone.

Dorian wept too. Julia comforted him by preening his hair. Ember roused from her slumber on my neck, *peeping* and nuzzling my cheek. The heat of her scales dried my tears, but they kept coming.

Grace is five foot nothing. Somehow she pulled us all into a group hug while murmuring about how we'd get through this. She knew all about grief from losing her parents. I wanted to rely on her experience, but my heart felt like it beat on the outside of my chest, raw and painful.

A few minutes later the teakettle whistled. Bubbe escorted us to the kitchen and poured boiling water over dried leaves. The aroma of tea had a universal and almost magical power.

Dorian sniffled, wiped his nose with the back of his hand, then grimaced and turned to wash them in the sink.

"Where's the Kleenex?" Logan glanced at the empty counter.

Bubbe set a box of tissues beside the tea tray. We blew our noses and dried our tears. Grace stopped crying first, then Logan, then me. Dorian ran out of tears last.

"Sorry." He blew his nose at the sink. "Mom said this was gonna hurt. Didn't want to believe her. But, well."

"Don't apologize for grief," Grace said.

"Thanks, then." Dorian sat down and poured tea. "It would have been worse if you all hadn't been here."

"Do you want to hear some good news?" Logan put sugar in his tea.

"Absotively."

He told Dorian all about the scholarship situation, with Grace adding a few details.

"Awesome." Dorian grinned. "I worried we'd be missing folks next year."

"We won't," Grace said. "Unless a certain situation goes sideways."

"What situation?" Logan blinked.

"Hal's."

Dorian cleared his throat. "Jonah's hearing is tomorrow, and I'm giving a statement. So we're staying at the hotel. Anything fun going on in town tonight?"

"There's a Piercing Whispers show at Dodge Street Café," I offered.

"How do we get there?" Dorian asked.

"We walk." Grace pulled her phone out and tapped out directions. "It's around the corner from Walgreens."

"Cool." Dorian checked his phone after it beeped. "I'll see you there. For now, we've got to check in at the hotel. Thanks again, you guys." He stood.

We left our tea behind and walked him out. His parents waited at the counter holding a check in the exact amount before Bubbe tallied their charge. Being clairvoyant had its perks.

The Dodge Street venue wasn't really a café. It was also a bar. The stage sat between the baristas and the bartenders, enough division for an all-ages gathering place. The bouncer checked our IDs and gave us wristbands at the door.

"This ruins my whole aesthetic." Dorian flicked the strip of neon green plastic.

"Looks cyber-goth to me." Grace snorted. "Neon green goes with black anyway."

"What do you know, K-pop Stan?" He chuckled.

Their banter was good-natured with no hard feelings, which couldn't be said about Dorian and Dylan. They had a sort of truce but still didn't like each other. Not even after last year.

They're jealous of each other. It's untenable.

I imagined why Dorian and Dylan needed to bury the hatchet. I hoped this next year would be easier, all things considered. However, the inside voice might be how my brain interpreted patterns of magic and coincidence. With practically his last breath, Professor Luciano said listen to the magic, even if it's harsh. Ignoring that would dishonor him.

"Is this it?" Logan glanced at empty seats.

"Don't worry," Grace said. "I think your sister's got that covered."

Brianna Collins walked through the door. She held it for an entourage. Brianna was one of Cadence's classmates at Gallows Hill, and she'd brought the entire extramural team, including Bar, Cadence, and Crow. After the last wolf shifter entered, she stayed put. Izzy led Lee, Hal, Faith, and Jacinda inside.

"Oh, that's good," Logan said. "You still need to talk to her about the thing."

"Is this the best time, though?"

"No. But maybe she'll meet you another day."

"What's this about?" Grace watched the door.

"Oh, I wanted some memory psychic help."

She's distracted.

"Cool." Grace stood on her tiptoes, trying to see over Crow's head. "Out of the way, featherbrain."

"Are you talking to me?" Crow narrowed his eyes.

Cadence put her hand on his arm. "Let her through."

Crow stepped aside.

Grace squealed and took off, dashing toward the door where a familiar face showed through the crowd.

Honestly, are you surprised?

"No. It makes sense."

"What?" Logan scratched his head.

"Grace and Azrael." I still hadn't told Logan about the inside voice.

"Is she trying to eat his face?" Logan grimaced. "He should watch his hands." He looked away.

"Found the virgin." Crow rolled his eyes.

"You found two." I glared, making fists. "You got a problem with that?"

Shut that fire off.

I banished the flames around my knuckles, but he'd seen them already.

"Um, no. It's fine, whatever, uh, doesn't float your boat. " He swallowed and edged away.

"Edgelords are so last year. You okay?" I patted Logan's shoulder.

"Yeah. I shouldn't have said that about Grace and Az. It was rude." He sighed. "They're the normal ones."

"I know what you mean." I nodded. "It's awkward for me too, watching public displays of affection."

Logan blinked as his mouth dropped open. For a moment, the muddled sound of several conversations acted like a white noise machine. Our eyes met. Had we ever locked gazes like this?

The first time you met. Last summer. And here you are again.

"Aliyah, are you a—"

"Hey." Izzy waved at us from the line at the coffee counter. "Come on, before they get swamped."

In line, we talked about the show, wondering what they'd play. Noah said they mostly did covers, but Logan mentioned they'd been practicing original stuff the last time he visited Elanor. Drinks in hand, we looked for seats. By that time, the place was packed. Most folks on the bar side were college kids from Salem State.

All mundane.

"I don't care."

"What?" Izzy blinked.

"Inside-outside voice problems again." I let out a nervous laugh.

"Did you want me to bring Jacinda over here?" Logan nodded toward where she stood by the door.

"No, they're about to start. I'll catch her after their set."

Piercing Whispers chose that moment to step onstage. Elanor switched her keyboard on. Dylan slung his Paul Reed Smith over his shoulder. Noah adjusted the mic stand. Arick sat behind the drum set. Some of the college kids snickered, probably because Arick had such a baby face.

"We're Piercing Whispers. Two, three, four." Noah cut the laughter off. Arick kicked off the beat as Dylan popped a riff, starting their first song.

At first, I didn't recognize the melody. That made sense because I'd never been a fan of The Cure. Piercing Whispers changed my mind about the post-punk band. *Push* had a long, uplifting introduction that showcased the band's teamwork. Logan got up and danced. People on both sides of the Dodge Street Café joined in.

Nobody snickered at Arick after such a strong open. As their set continued, so did the dancing. Even the bartender and baristas rocked out while pouring and brewing.

Their last song was *Nine In The Afternoon* by Panic! At The Disco. Logan dragged me up to dance with him. We weren't formal like at Hawthorn, but I found myself able to keep up. Somehow, he'd taught me to dance without really trying.

At the end of the set, most everyone cheered. As the crowd quieted, I headed straight toward the door, where Jacinda still stood. As I approached, her eyes widened.

"Hi there, I'm—"

"Yeah, Aliyah Morgenstern. I know." She blinked. "Why are you here?"

"I recognized you from extramurals. You led the Messing cheer squad, right?"

"Yeah, but what do you want with me?" She leaned against the wall like she wanted to merge with it.

You're scaring her. You know that, right?

My heart didn't feel it, but my mind shouldn't forget that I scared some people.

"Logan says a lot of nice things about you."

"I thought you were classmates." Her shoulders eased a little. "Didn't realize you guys were a thing."

"He's one of my best friends. Anyway, it was nice to meet you. Sorry if I spooked you."

"I'm okay. Talk to you some other time, I guess."

"Yeah, don't be a stranger."

I sat back down at the table I shared with Logan, Izzy, and Lee, shaking my head.

"I told you to let me introduce you." Izzy sighed. "Jacinda's jumpy around strangers to begin with, and you were the tough gal on campus last year."

"I didn't feel tough."

"The rumors say you fought Tempe in a room full of vampires, saved Dorian, and survived a lethal attack." Izzy sighed again. "I know what really happened and still think you're a badass."

"I'll reintroduce you," Logan said.

By that time, Jacinda was nowhere in sight.

I stood outside the courthouse on Federal Street with Noah the next night, along with Dad, Logan, and Dorian with his parents. Because Jonah was a vampire, the Night Court handled this case.

"It's only a hearing." Mr. Spanos said.

"But it's important." Noah sighed. "This is where they decide whether the cases are connected."

"That's not right." I swallowed the urge to conjure fire. "They are. All three of us were there."

"The judge doesn't know that." Mrs. Spanos said. "The bones gave me no sure answer, and my auguries were unclear."

"The truth will out." Dorian nodded. "At least that's what I keep telling myself."

"Hoo." Julia preened his hair.

Our group was the first inside the courthouse's expensive lobby. We walked through the second set of thick wooden doors on the left. The bailiff already stood beside the judge's chambers. The court reporter tapped her device with a wand. I watched raptly. Wand magic was college-level work.

Minutes later, a diminutive white-haired man with twinkling brown eyes and beige skin walked through the door. He set a briefcase on the defendant's side, opened it, then sat. He must be Jonah's lawyer.

"That's Yoshi Ichiro, from Providence," Dad murmured. "Your mother met him in Providence two years ago."

"Is he any good?" Noah asked.

"One of the best." Dorian sighed. "The other guy's better."

The man sauntering toward the prosecutor's table had a grin like a thousand knives. I read the name on his ID badge, which also stated his registry status and legal credentials. Slade Sharpe was a shark shifter and had alphabet soup after his name.

I hope the defense has more witnesses.

Another bailiff escorted Jonah to sit with Mr. Ichiro. I glanced over my shoulder and spotted familiar faces. Alex Onassis wore a suit with a bow tie, not his usual choice of attire, but appropriate if he meant to give a statement. He sat beside a man about Bubbe's age, who I'd never seen before.

Behind them sat Arick Magnuson, alone and also wearing a tie and jacket.

So, he came to town for more than a gig.

"All rise."

The judge entered, and everyone stood. Before she sat, the door opened once again behind me, and Temperance Fairbanks walked through, flanked by her father and her older sister Charity. Faith was nowhere in sight. I hoped she was still at Hawthorn with Hal.

"Be seated," the bailiff directed.

The hearing started. From what I understood, they were trying to determine whether Jonah wanted to turn Noah or if there was a chance he'd been coerced. The judge took a written statement from Temperance.

Of course, she denies it all.

Arick handed over a magisupremacist pamphlet against vampires and anyone who accepted them, stating she'd given it to him last fall.

The judge perused it with a raised eyebrow and set it on top of Temperance's statement. I crossed my fingers in my lap, hoping that meant she considered it more important.

Dorian handed over his account next. He hadn't seen much, only a little before he got knocked out. I saw the page as he carried it up. It referred to Alex, which explained why he was here.

When Alex rose to give his statement, his hands were empty. The man with him stood at his side, holding a magipsychic device I recognized as a lie detector. The judge shook her head.

"Only written statements at this time, Mr. Onassis. You have two hours to compose remarks. "

"Miss Fairbanks, your statement please."

She spoke to Charity, who stepped forward with an entire folder full of papers.

Once again, the judge shook her head.

"This is excessive. Statements must be no more than three pages. You also have two hours. I suggest you edit them." The judge tapped her gavel. "Two-hour recess." She rose and exited through the door to her chambers.

The man with Alex sat, shaking his head. Dad stood and spoke to him.

"It must be confusing, navigating a whole new legal system."

"Yes." He nodded. "Is different." His voice was heavily accented.

"The most important thing to do is summarize, highlight incidents related to the specific charge."

"Hmm." The man sighed.

I wondered where Alex's parents were.

They sided with the Fairbanks. He's here against their wishes.

"I've got this." Dorian strode down the aisle toward them.

Alex widened his eyes and dropped his pen. Julia swooped down to retrieve it and held the writing implement out to him in one talon. Then something unexpected happened.

Dorian explained everything in Greek. His parents grinned approvingly at their son.

The man smiled. "This makes sense now." He rattled off several points in his native tongue, using his fingers to count. Alex nodded and began writing his statement.

"That's Alex's cousin, Konstantin. Did you know Alex's father is an earl?" Dorian whispered from his seat after he'd returned.

"No." I blinked.

Bet Alex's mother married him for the title.

"He needed more information." Dorian smirked. "Neither of them understood the legalese."

"My son, the future lawyer." Mrs. Spanos smiled.

"Who can argue with a clairvoyant?" Everyone chuckled at Dad's joke.

"Looks like the other side's having a harder time."

Temperance and Charity squabbled over her statements as their mother ignored them. Unsurprising considering everything Faith had said about her family.

They finished before the two hours were up, so the bailiff informed the judge, who emerged a few minutes later. After they handed over their documents, the judge announced that she'd make her decision tomorrow at sunset.

The hearing ended. Noah leaned forward before the bailiff came to lead Jonah away.

"We'll get through this," he said.

"We?" Jonah kept his back turned. "There is no we, Noah."

"What?" My brother clutched the lapel over his heart. "You can't mean that."

"I advise you to discontinue this conversation, Mr. Arnold," Mr. Ichiro said.

"Come on Arnold, back to your cell." The bailiff clipped a chain around the shackles on Jonah's wrist, then yanked it.

Without another word, the bailiff led him from the room.

"Can I stay in my old room, Dad?" Noah asked. "Just for tonight?"

"Sure." Dad put his arm around him. "It's still sunproof."

The entire walk home, Noah was silent. Once inside, he headed immediately toward his room and shut the door. I followed, but he didn't answer when I knocked. Later, when I got in bed to sleep, my brother still sobbed on the other side of the wall.

The next day, Noah stayed until we heard the news, which was good. The judge considered Jonah's case to be part of Tempe's and sent him home to await the trial in the winter.

But no matter how many times Noah called or texted, Jonah didn't answer.

CHAPTER FOUR

"What do you want to do for your birthday, Logan?" Dad asked.

"Oh, I almost forgot it was August." He smiled down at Doris, who purred in his lap on the sofa in the living room. "I'm not sure. Nothing big, though. Maybe pizza with friends."

"I can round everyone up," I offered.

"Yeah, let's do that." He glanced up. For one brief shining moment, our eyes met. His smile nearly broke my heart. I wasn't sure why.

You care for him. Deeply.

That truth was like the back of Bar's truck on the day Noah moved. Full of stuff that needed unpacking. Eventually.

I texted Izzy, Cadence, Brianna, Noah—everyone who wasn't on Hawthorn's campus. Gathering everyone from campus meant I had to go out since they didn't have phone service. I left him with the *Encyclopedia of Magical Creatures*, Bubbe's birthday present. Which reminded me, I ought to do some shopping. I'd managed to save enough for what I hoped was the perfect gift.

On the street, I turned down Essex, searching for the door to Hawthorn Academy. This year I wasn't on probation or banned from entering campus, but I hadn't had much time to visit there. I'd only gone once to swim in the baths with Faith and Izzy back in June.

The door was beside the bank this time. In summer, you had to knock unless you were living on campus. Penelope answered. She gave out to-go bags at dinnertime. My smile faded, and my excitement leaked away. Her face looked stretched and weary.

This does not bode well. Find out what's rotten.

"Penelope, what's wrong?"

"There's been an unexpected—" she started.

"Aliyah." Hal peered over her shoulder. I hadn't seen him since June, and he'd grown. He'd been shorter than her a few months ago. "Come in. I've got this, Mrs. Andros."

They stepped aside to let me through, but neither spoke. Hal led me to the stairs and called out our floor, leaving Penelope behind.

"Hal, what's going—"

"In a minute." He held a finger over his lips and leaned on the banister.

"You grew." I changed the subject.

"Yeah, up mostly, but a little out." He grinned but not with his eyes. "Wouldn't call it a glow-up but square's a better shape than round, am I right?"

He was. Hal Hawkins had always been husky, but the added height had transformed him from bulky to imposing.

"You could be Bar's stunt double." I waved a hand at his shoulders. "You're almost as tall as me now. Is it from your magiglobular anemia?"

"The air's super thin up here." He deflected. "Why didn't you warn me?" His banter was a band-aid on a bullet wound.

We walked down the hall to the room he shared with Lee, who wasn't inside when he opened the door. Hal's father sat at the foot of his bed. Instead of a suit, he wore the teacher's version of the school blazer over khakis and a polo shirt.

"Miss Morgenstern." He stood and straightened the blazer. "You may as well hear it straight for me."

"Hear what?"

"The trustees found a loophole in my terms." He paced. "They didn't choose a replacement from my list. Instead, they reinstated a former headmaster. My father, to be exact."

His face wore the grimmest expression I'd seen on it since Hal's diagnosis. This wasn't good news.

It's bad. But not as awful as it could've been, I suppose.

"How can I help, Professor?"

"By minding his rules, even the ones that seem absurd." He sighed. "My father's tenure was well-established by the time your parents attended Hawthorn. They likely have stories. However, there's something you specifically should know."

"What is it?"

"I became headmaster because my father was under suspicion of aiding and abetting your uncle, Richard Hopewell." He faced Hal. "Furthermore, my mother was also involved."

"Nana?" Hal tilted his head. "Why?"

"She's a djinn, pledged to her lamp not long after you started kindergarten. You'll learn this in class, but all lamp-bound djinn serve three terms with three wishes each. On her first term, Richard held her lamp."

"She's done horrible things, then." Hal's hands curled into fists. "Murderous things."

"She couldn't help it, I thought?" I put a hand on Hal's shoulder. "Djinn have to obey."

"There's no way to ascertain whether she was reluctant." Professor Hawkins sighed. "Although I'd love to think she was. The court only ordered a list of wishes, not her opinions on them."

"I get why you want *me* to know this, but Aliyah?"

"Because her lamp's recently arrived on campus. I don't know who brought it." He leaned against the wall by the door. "If it's the wrong person, there will be trouble."

"What if Grandpa's got it, though?" Hal asked.

"That's not so bad but still dangerous." Professor Hawkins sighed. "He's holding an enormous grudge against Richard for exploiting my mother's lamp. Which extends to Aliyah."

We watched Nin chase Ember across the floor.

"You both should be on guard. I'd advise against anyone in her family attending school events in the near future, including Parent's Night."

"What if someone else has the lamp?" I hugged myself, shivering all of a sudden. "Do we have to worry about Temperance-level problems, I mean?"

"Headmaster Hawkins will stick to the official rules of the school, no matter who breaks them. And his space magic is far stronger than mine. He'll respond to threats much faster than I was able to."

Did he just refer to his father as Headmaster Hawkins? Family drama on display isn't his usual look.

"I still don't understand." I shook my head. "Why tell me all this?"

"I'm telling you both." He sighed. "Our families built this school together, connected to it by generations of magic. You've each helped defend it in your ways. You might have to step up again."

"I'm not afraid to fight." Hal pressed his lips together.

"I am. But that hasn't stopped me before."

"That's all I can reasonably expect. Thank you both." Professor Hawkins strode toward the door, opened it, and left. The tension went out of the room with him.

"Well, that was intense." I blinked. "Are you okay?"

"I will be. Anyway, you had your reasons for coming to campus, and I totally hijacked you."

"I'm on a mission." I sighed. "It's Logan's birthday."

"Oh my God, I almost forgot." Hal chuckled. "Are you throwing him a party?"

"Some covert shopping and taking him to Engine House at eight. He wanted me to invite you and Faith. Everyone on campus and our friends in town, is what he said."

"Are you sure he meant everybody?"

"I think so?"

"Because Alex is on campus. Has been since July."

"Really?"

"Yeah." He nodded. "Cousin Konstantin went back to Greece last week, and he moved in here. By the way, is Noah okay? I haven't seen him since that hearing."

"The first night he took it really hard. Came back to our house instead of going to his apartment. He's ghosting me now."

"Dylan says Noah's throwing himself into music. He's worried."

"I'm here for him. If only he'd say something."

"It's hard." Hal nodded. "Faith spent almost every day in the gym and the baths. I've never seen her this angry."

"Is she okay?"

"She's bringing Seth to Bubbe's for his check-up later. Working out helps her cope. Her father sent her a letter. He's moving into the faculty wing in September."

"Why?"

"Trustees have the right to take residence while school's in session. Almost all of them have moved things in already."

"Wow." I blinked.

"I hope Grandpa gives them strict guidelines."

"So he's a rules guy?"

"Major disciplinarian, letter of the law. No wonder he married a Seelie djinn. Anyway, you said you're shopping?"

"Yeah, for Logan."

"What are you getting him?"

"No idea." I shrugged. "Are you up for a stroll through town?"

"Yeah, actually." He grinned. "Nice thing about this growth spurt, I cover more ground with less effort. I need to drop the invites in the tubes on the way out."

Before I could ask how he'd managed to make invitations while sitting there chatting, he pulled them from under the device on his desk.

"Is that what you've been doing all summer? Making that?" I jerked my thumb at the squat wood and metal box.

"It's a perpetual printer. Never runs out of ink. Lee and Faith helped me enchant it."

"Where's the manual?"

"There isn't one outside my head." He beamed while holding one of the invitations toward me. "I invented it."

I stood and peered at the paper. It had all the information about Logan's birthday, printed in a purple so dark it was almost black. I glanced back at the unassuming device.

"Wow, this is amazing. Does it work with computers? Magipsychic displays?"

"Yes and yes." Hal chuckled. "Dad hated trying to order ink in here. Mail order is tricky because the front door's always moving. So, I figured at least Grandpa won't have the same problem."

"Butter him up, is that it?"

"I can neither confirm nor deny that." He winked. "But kindness never hurts."

Except when it does.

"Anyway, let's go." I grinned while swallowing the voice's naysaying. "Logan's gift isn't going to pick itself."

Out in town, Hal kept up with me easily. I could pretend he wasn't sick, never had magiglobular anemia. Almost. Because he paused a little too long in front of some of the windows and leaned more heavily against counters and walls than I might have.

Nothing in the shops along the walking-only section of Essex Street felt special enough for Logan's birthday gift. That's why we crossed Washington Street, Crombie, and Summer Street toward the Salem Athenaeum.

It was the oldest book repository in town. To mundane society, it was a treasure trove of genealogical, trade, and city records. For extrahumans, it was more. The basement catacombs contained the area's magical histories. Even Boston couldn't boast this comprehensive a collection, in large part because the Salem Athenaeum's records predated colonial times.

We only planned to stop for a break from the heat in a building with climate control, but we walked right into their semi-annual antique fundraiser.

I sifted halfheartedly through jewelry and knickknacks, then moved on to a small shelf of books. I ran my fingers along the spines but stopped after feeling a brief jolt of energy. I pulled the item under my hand from the shelf. I mistook it for a book at first since it was bound in pebbled leather until Hal pointed out the clasps along the top and bottom.

"Is that a box?" Hal blinked. "What's inside?"

"I don't know." I opened the clasps.

When I lifted the lid, time seemed to stop. A lustrously bristled brush rested between pots of color, unfaded and still full despite the wooden housing's obvious age.

"This is it."

"You've seen paints in five other shops already today though," Hal countered.

This is no ordinary paint set. You know it.

"This one's an antique." I swallowed, suddenly reluctant to mention the jolt I'd gotten. "It's got history. Logan loves that kind of thing."

"I'm rooting for you." Hal held his hands up, crossing fingers on both hands. "It might be more than you can afford, though."

It wasn't. When I brought the box of paints to the woman sitting at the table with the cash box, she declared its price as eighty-five dollars, almost exactly what I'd saved over the summer.

"Are you an artist?" she asked.

"No, it's for a friend." I scrounged in my bag for the last few bits of change. "It's his birthday."

"Your boyfriend?" She winked at Hal.

"My best friend," I confirmed. "It's a surprise."

She put the gift in a brown paper bag, and that was that.

Once outside the Athenaeum, we headed back down toward the center of town.

"I thought Izzy was your bestie." Hal elbowed me.

"Um." Despite the August heat, my cheeks blazed.

"Logan's a special guy," he agreed. "Best friend isn't an absolute anyway. You can have more than one."

"Do you want to see if Faith's still at Bubbe's?" I studied his face, checking for signs of fatigue. "Or maybe go back to campus and rest?"

"Bubbe's sounds great."

I blinked and stopped in the middle of the sidewalk. He glanced over his shoulder, then paced back toward me.

"Look, I didn't feel up to leaving campus for months. Ever since this growth spurt, I feel downright normal." Hal gave me a lopsided grin. "I don't know if that makes sense."

"It does." I nodded. "I'm happy for you."

We continued down Essex to the door of the school. I nodded at it, but Hal shook his head. He wasn't even winded. Ember swooped off my shoulder. Hal chuckled as Nin scampered down his arm, then hopped on her back. My dragonet flew with her passenger the rest of the way down Essex, around the corner, along Hawthorne Street, and up our driveway.

She landed on the front step in front of Bubbe's office, where Nin jumped off and excitedly squeaked while waving her front paws in circles. She hopped up and down a few times while chattering excitedly at Hal. He smiled and scooped her up into his arms, then stroked the top of her head.

"This is a good day." Hal beamed.

"With any luck, it'll only get better." I smiled back.

"I'm going to see how Faith is doing."

"This needs wrapping upstairs." I shook the paper bag. "I'll be down soon."

He entered the veterinary office while I headed into my apartment. I ran up both flights of stairs, gulping down air like I ran laps at the school gym. I huffed and puffed, struggling to wrap Logan's gift in brightly colored paper. I debated putting a bow on it, but then someone knocked at my bedroom door.

"Just a sec!" I jumped up, swept the gift under my bed, and threw the empty bag into my closet before closing the door.

"Aliyah?"

"Come in, Mom."

"Is everything okay?"

"I was wrapping a, um, birthday present." I chuckled. "For Logan."

"Oh?" Mom raised an eyebrow.

"I'm not breathing a word about what's in it. Doris hears everything, and it's a surprise."

"I understand." Mom nodded. "The letter came from—"

"Hiram Hawkins. He's the new headmaster. Hal told me. We hung out today."

"Oh. Well, that's a relief." She sighed. "Did he say anything about what Hiram is like?"

"No, but his father did." I told her everything I remembered about my conversation with Hal's dad.

"Interesting." Mom leaned in the doorway and pondered her next words. "I suppose there are pros and cons to having him back. Although, I had hoped Nancy Gauthier would have been their choice."

"Gauthier? Why does that name sound familiar?"

"Nancy's got long experience on staff at Weir Academy up in Niagara. Her presence might have proved restorative. Especially with Andre Gauthier on the Board of Trustees here. They're siblings."

"That would have been nice, I guess. But for now, everything's a mess."

"Perhaps so. It gets better, I promise."

"I'm not sure it will." I told her what Hal said about Faith's father living on campus.

"I need to make some calls, Aliyah. Don't be alarmed."

"You rush off to make phone calls and tell me not to be alarmed?"

"Yes. What I discover in those phone calls is more important than the fact I'm making them. If you've got cause to worry, I'll let you know."

"Okay."

I trusted her but knew nothing about her sources. My mother's back retreated down the hall. Once she turned the corner and descended the stairs, I followed slowly. By the time I reached the first floor of our apartment, she was already in her office with the door closed.

While heading down to Bubbe's, I decided not to tell my friends about Mom's concerns until I had the whole story.

CHAPTER FIVE

Logan opened the door, placed one finger over his lips, then pointed at the kitchen entrance. I nodded, jerked my thumb over my shoulder toward the stairs, and raised my eyebrow. Logan nodded so we headed back upstairs and sat on stools at the kitchen counter.

"Seth's checkup is over. Faith's having counseling. Hal's in there, but we shouldn't be." Logan got a banana from the fruit basket and peeled it.

"Makes sense." I took an apple, held it, and stared instead of taking a bite. I put it back, suddenly not hungry.

Those unknown phone calls are spoiling your appetite. Go and insist on listening in.

"I'll talk to her again."

"Faith?"

"Sorry, inside voice came out." I grimaced. "Mom."

"About school stuff?" He blinked.

"Maybe."

"She told you about Hal's grandfather, didn't she?"

"Yes. But there's something else. Something harder to deal with."

"Do you need a test run?" He broke off a banana chunk and popped

57

it into his mouth, where it comically muffled his voice. "I can talk just fine."

He looked like a hamster with his cheeks full of fruit, so I giggled.

"What?" He blinked, then widened his eyes and puffed his cheeks out even more.

I held my sides, laughing too much for speech, reveling in the broken tension. In typical Logan fashion, he made things better by being himself.

There's a typical Logan fashion now? How interesting.

I recovered from my mirth enough to pat his shoulder, but I was still too breathless to speak. Or sit up straight. He set the banana on the counter and caught me as I toppled from the stool. We ended up hugging.

His longer than usual hair brushed against my cheek, soft and ticklish, like Doris's whiskers. All my worry about Mom's covert conversations in the other room melted away.

"Thanks, Logan." I leaned back. "Maybe I needed a hug."

"Hugging works for Elanor." Logan glanced down and to the side.

You've seen that before.

I kept my mouth shut, thinking my question at the voice. *When?*

All the time.

"Would you mind if I finished that?" Logan nodded at the half-eaten fruit.

"Not a bit." I let go of him, grinning.

After that, I went to the fridge for lemonade. He followed, so I poured a glass for us both. By the time we finished our drinks, Bubbe had opened the door from the stairs and beckoned.

We followed her down and into the kitchen, where Faith and Hal sat with the remains of their tea in front of them, Nin and Seth curled up in the corner. Logan stopped in the doorway, staring at Hal with his mouth open. Apparently, he hadn't seen him come in. They had a conversation off in the corner about the amazing growth spurt.

"Are you coming to Engine House? I asked Faith.

"Wouldn't miss it." She nodded. "It'll be good to get off campus and do something."

"You haven't come out for Piercing Whispers, though."

"Hal wasn't feeling up to it. But over the last couple of weeks, he's had way more energy."

"More energy?" Bubbe tilted her head. "Was that before or after the growth spurt?"

"Hmm." Faith stacked teacups and saucers on the tray as she thought. "I think just after. He was still tired when I noticed I could put my head on his shoulder without leaning. After that, he started running in the gym with me. He's still slower than Coach Chen's tortoise, though."

"Noted," Bubbe said.

I didn't like her flat expression or the appraising glance she gave Hal on her way to the sink with the tea things. Surely she'd noticed his height already, but his newfound energy concerned my grandmother enough for her to mask her reaction.

"I've got another appointment coming in, so you kids ought to head out. Enjoy your special day, Logan."

We nodded, smiled, and bid her farewell on the way out the door. Standing around in the driveway, we tried to decide how to kill time.

In the end, we knocked on Izzy's door, but she wasn't there. Her *abuela* said she'd gone to Hawthorn with Lee. We found the entry on Essex Street and went inside. Hal went upstairs to find Lee. The rest of us went into the café, ordered lattes, and sat drinking them in the lounge together.

"Morgenstern. What are you doing here?" The voice was more haughty than hostile. I turned to find my ex-boyfriend standing over us, his basilisk hissing at us from his shoulder.

"Hey, Alex." Logan spoke to the magus but looked at his familiar instead. "I'm going out for my birthday. Want to come along?"

"You're not seriously asking me to some boring nerd party?" Alex blinked.

"It's just pizza. But yeah. I am." Doris chirped at his feet for good measure.

"I'm busy. But I guess it's a nice thought." Alex walked up to the counter, then around it, where he pulled an apron off the hook and tied it on. He narrowed his eyes. "Don't act like you've never seen work-study."

None of us knew how to react. Alex Onassis was the last person anyone expected to need financial aid. His mother was a trustee, his father nobility. He'd also disparaged Dylan for standing behind that same counter.

However, Faith, Hal, and Logan hadn't been at the hearing. They didn't know only his barely bilingual cousin had accompanied him.

He's had trouble at home.

Should I tell them? I thought at the inside voice.

It's not your story.

Hal returned.

"They're here but doing, um, some projects right now." His eyes moved from the floor to the table to the wall and the ceiling before settling on the floor again. "Anyway, we've got some time to kill before Engine House."

"I wonder if Creatives is open?" Logan pondered. "I haven't painted at all this summer."

"It is, but I haven't gone." Faith shrugged.

"Maybe we should make some art," I suggested.

Logan led us all down to the academic wing and into the Creatives room, where we spent time engaged in arts and craft projects. Our familiars played in the corner.

I'd arrived at Engine House before everyone else last summer. This year, we walked in to find the section in the back entirely marked off and halfway occupied. Elanor waved us over and ushered Logan toward a seat decorated with balloons.

"Peep!"

Ember flew in circles around the floating rubber orbs, careful not to touch them. Gale warbled and took off from Dylan's shoulder to join her.

"Wow." He blinked. "Thanks. I would have been happy with plain old pizza."

"You only turn eighteen once." She shrugged. "Anyway, Brianna made assistant manager last week. So she helped me with this whole birthday scheme."

"Scheme?" I raised an eyebrow.

"The second she knew the location, El made a plan," Noah said.

We shuffled around and searched for seats, which wasn't easy. The section was packed. Cadence sat with Crow and Bar in one corner, laughing over one of her mom's newspaper articles. Lee had his familiar Scratch on his lap, where the sumxu sat up, flopping his lop ears while twitching his whiskers. Izzy filmed the critter's antics with her phone.

Grace sat nearby, oblivious to just about everything besides Azrael. In moments, she climbed into his lap, and they put their arms around each other. He whispered something in her ear that made her blush.

I let Hal and Faith sit together, which meant I got stuck in a corner, wedged between Crow and Lee, who both had bony shoulders. My comfort didn't matter. This was Logan's day.

Brianna brought pizzas and pitchers out, assisted by a coworker I'd never met. We ate, drank, and socialized. Logan made it a point to grin at me from across the table more than once. The third time, I noticed something outside the window behind him.

No, someone.

Sure enough, it was Jonah Arnold out there, walking with a redheaded woman who closely resembled him, which made sense. After the hearing, the bailiff hadn't led him back to jail.

He glanced over his shoulder, eyes widening when he spotted Noah. Who, thankfully, didn't see him. The woman with him shook her head and tugged his arm. She looked to be my parents' age. Was that his mom?

Jonah caught me looking. He made a zipping motion across his lips and walked on. I nodded, agreeing with what I thought he meant. That it'd be better for Noah not to know he'd been there.

You're taking on an awful lot of burdens for other people lately. After literally saving lives so recently. What exactly do you think you owe them?

"Nothing."

"Huh?" Crow glanced over his shoulder. "You talkin' to me?"

"Um, no."

"Good."

"She's cool." Bar snorted. "Hey, Aliyah."

"Hey, yourself." I snorted back to stay in the spirit of things.

"What are we now, kelpies?"

I laughed, deliberately making it sound like a whinny.

"Cornball troll." Crow rolled his eyes.

"That's Mr. Cornball to you, pal." I raised an eyebrow. "And don't you forget it."

Cadence threw back her head and laughed. Crow sighed and shook his head. Then he looked at his watch. I blinked.

"Gotta go." He twisted his shoulders somehow, then untangled himself from the row of seats.

"Aww." Cadence pouted. "All work and no play makes Crow a boring boyfriend."

"So dump me again." He smirked.

"I'd rather do this." She stood and kissed him, wrapping her arms around him under the trench coat he wore even on the sultry August night.

Her response utterly confused me. Not because I couldn't recognize Crow's sarcasm. But because I couldn't imagine anything like it being endearing in a romantic context.

"Thinks he's Han Solo." Bar shook his head. "Maybe he's not wrong."

"What do you mean?" I was glad to have a distraction from Cadence's long goodbye.

"He's a Merlini."

"Hmm." I nodded and closed my eyes around the sting of tears as I remembered one of Professor Luciano's more memorable lectures about Salem. "Rum runners. Prohibition, right?"

"Hey. You okay?"

"I'll live." I opened my eyes. "I guess you've got a point. Families have room for variety."

Like the birthday boy. And Faith.

Being reminded of my friends and how they'd survived boosted my mood.

"Yeah. His kid sister's their straight and narrow." Bar sighed. "Wish I'd rubbed off on him more, though."

"I hear you." I thought of Alex.

"Look, more root beer."

Bar pointed, nearly clunking his elbow into the side of my head. Ember swooped down from where she'd been perched beside Gale and *peeped* at him scoldingly. I laughed into my hands while Bar guffawed and slapped his knees. Ember hovered in the air, blinking at us. Then she circled back and landed next to Gale again. Their tails hung down and waved momentarily before twisting together.

They're holding hands, essentially.

"Cute." Bar jerked his chin at the dragonets.

"Yeah." I nodded, my throat suddenly tight.

"How'd it go, by the way? With that guy last year?"

"Nowhere, but we're cool being friends." I realized where Bar was trying to go with this. "I'm cool being friends with everyone, pretty much."

"Oh." He reached across the table and tipped the root beer pitcher over his cup. "So, who's pretty much?"

"Um." My face felt like I'd run ten laps around the gym. "I mean I can't imagine myself doing anything like that."

I glanced at Grace and Azrael, still intertwined together on one seat, their pizza entirely ignored. Cadence chose that moment to sit back down and lean in front of Bar while raising her eyebrow.

"What in the world did you say to my friend, Bartholomew?"

"Don't look at me." He shrugged. "It's Ambersmith's fault."

"I suppose their PDA pushes the bounds of R-rated." Cadence shook her head. "Seriously, Aliyah. You go to boarding school. Surely you've seen stuff like that before."

I ignored her and focused on finishing my now tepid pizza. At least the Sprite in my cup was still cold and fizzy. Bar followed suit. Cadence's banter was usually harmless, but it had never made me feel this uncomfortable before.

By the time I set my pizza crust down, the lights had dimmed. I glanced at Logan, who looked a little lost at the head of the table. Almost like he was alone in the crowd. The lighting change must have surprised him but not too much. A moment later, Elanor started singing Happy Birthday and Brianna came out of the back carrying a large sheet cake, decorated with the words "Happy Birthday, Logan" and eighteen candles on top.

Logan looked at Elanor, smiling. Right then, I thought he wished for peace in his family. When he turned to blow the candles out, he glanced at me, and I wasn't sure. After putting the candles aside, Brianna used one of the semicircular pizza slicers to cut the cake. Inside it was vanilla with vanilla frosting, Logan's favorite. I ended up with a piece that had half his name on it.

After the cake, Brianna shooed us out because Engine House was closing. Outside, friends exchanged hugs along with promises we'd see each other again soon. They trailed away in small groups or pairs. Elanor, Noah, Logan, and I lingered. At first, I thought they stalled to invite us over. When Brianna shut the lights off inside the restaurant and came out, I realized something else was going on.

"Okay, I'm ready to hear that new song." Brianna stepped beside Elanor and grabbed her hand. She glanced over her shoulder before crossing Derby Street. "Happy birthday again, Logan."

"Thanks." He scooped a sleepy Doris up in his arms. "Can we go, Aliyah? I'm tired."

"Sure."

I started down Derby with him. Ember landed on my shoulder and curled around my neck, also exhausted. Was I the only one with any energy left?

You're nervous.

I couldn't imagine why.

The gift. And me. You were going to tell him.

"Do you think you could stay up a little longer? After we get back, I mean."

"Maybe." He glanced at me. "Why?"

"I've got something for you."

"Oh, you shouldn't have. I didn't get you anything back in June, and that's bad manners."

"Logan." I stopped and stepped in front of him. "In my family, we give gifts because we care, not to get something back."

"Wow." He blinked. "Well, lead on then."

I did. After another minute, we stood in front of my house.

"Do you want to come up?"

"Um—" He swallowed and stared at the entrance to Bubbe's office.

"Never mind. I have to go upstairs to get it. Can we meet on the back porch?"

"Oh, okay." He nodded, shoulders easing.

We went through separate doors. After climbing up two flights of stairs, swapping a sleepy Ember for the package, and descending again, I still wasn't tired. My legs burned slightly with the exertion, though. Out on the back porch, Logan stood staring up at the moon.

"Hi." I stepped toward him. "Where's Doris?"

"Wouldn't budge after camping out on my pillow." He grinned while glancing sideways and down again. "Is it a laser pointer?"

"Hmm?"

"The, um, gift?" He sighed, turned toward the porch railing, and gripped it as though he needed support.

"Well, no." I blinked. "You don't have to answer, but what made you guess that?"

"Just how stuff like that usually is." His knuckles whitened in the moonlight. "Bubbe's the only person who gave me something, well, for me. Must be some kind of world record for that, huh? Being given stuff someone else would want for seventeen years."

"I don't know about that." I brought the hastily-wrapped package out from behind my back. "Maybe you get to break a personal record because I saw this and instantly knew it belonged with you." I held it out. "Happy birthday, Logan."

When his hands let go of the railing, they shook. Not in a trembling way, either. He was flapping them, what Mom referred to as a self-stimulatory behavior. While I'd heard him hum through tests and schoolwork, I hadn't seen him do one physically before.

You have with his nails. Anyway, you know what to do.

I nodded, waiting. I wish I could say Logan took it in stride, but his face reddened, jaw dropped and eyes wide and feral. Tears gathered at their corners. Mine stung, too. Mom always said this is a natural response to excitement for folks on the spectrum. The Pierces either hadn't gotten that memo or knew and shamed him for it.

The latter. They're horrible.

Afterward, he turned his back. "I'm sorry. You can go if you want to."

"I'm not going anywhere."

"Why?"

"This is your normal, Logan. Like the fire and solar are mine. You accepted that about me the minute you saw it. Why shouldn't I do the same?"

"You saved my life that day." He turned his head enough for me to see him in profile. "I did...that...in the middle of you doing me a favor."

"Eighteen's a big deal, especially away from home. It's an exodus of sorts, nothing to sneeze at."

"I'm ashamed."

"Whatever happens, I'm here."

"Okay." He sniffled and drew his sleeve across his face under his eyes.

When he turned, tears still silvered parts of his face. He looked strange and fae in the moonlight, but not alarmingly so.

Some people have a hard streak, like tinfoil wedged into the heel of a loaf of babka. Inside Logan Pierce lived a profound gentleness, one that wouldn't have survived if he hadn't encased it in a lumpy and sometimes awkward shell.

I silently thanked God that he'd spent an entire year thriving here instead of withering in Las Vegas. When I held the parcel out this time, he took it.

Instead of ripping the paper, Logan peeled the tape on the edges and along the seam. He managed to unwrap it without making a single tear, grinning the entire time. Some of my schoolmates were defenders, like Faith and I. Others were creators, like Grace and Hal. Logan was something else entirely. "A conservator."

"No, it's a book." He stared down at the leather-bound box. "Wait. No, it's not."

I memorized his face, trying to imprint every detail of his expression as his fingers traced the spine, navigated the corner, and found the first latch.

"A box that looks like a book!" He smiled. "I always wanted one of these. Thank you!"

"There's something inside."

He opened it, the contents striking him speechless.

"Oh, Aliyah." His voice dropped half an octave in pitch. "This is too beautiful. I almost can't—" He sniffled again, closed the box, and set it on the railing.

My shoulders felt tingly all of a sudden. My lip trembled, vision doubling then blurring over. Before I knew it, we were both in tears and in each other's arms, exactly like that night in Noah's apartment three months earlier.

"I gave what I thought you'd want," I said behind his ear.

"You do too much for me, Aliyah." His hands pressed flat against my back, different from how they did every other time we'd hugged.

"You deserve it."

"If you say so."

"I know so."

We disengaged, studied each other's tear-stained faces for scant moments, then walked inside. He parted from me in the stairwell, his free hand a silhouette waving shyly in the light of Bubbe's hallway.

I'd forgotten something but couldn't think of what. When I ascended the stairs, barely feeling them under my feet, I couldn't imagine why. Despite my attempts to ask my inside voice, it didn't respond.

CHAPTER SIX

It should have felt all wrong, walking to Hawthorn without Noah. But Logan's presence made it better, if not exactly right. We began making our goodbyes to my parents and to Bubbe, who'd come with us. She handed me an old medical case, not large.

"What's this?" I studied its battered nylon surface.

"A brooding box."

"Whoa!" Logan beamed. "I'll help you set it up if you want. This is awesome! Do you think Ember's going to lay eggs?"

"Peep?"

My dragonet craned her neck down, flaring her nostrils at the case. Then, she turned her head and started preening my hair. Or at least that's what I thought she was doing at first.

"Ow!" I winced, reflexively ducking my head. Anyone would have if they'd had several strands of hair yanked out. "I have a hairbrush I always forget to clean, you know."

"That's a nesting behavior, so I'd say she's either ready or will be in a few months." Bubbe nodded. "She'll be on campus with a male about her age, too. I want you to be prepared."

"Okay." I nodded, trying to keep my expression neutral. I'd heard rumors. The prospect of feeling amorous via my familiar bond was pretty close to horrifying. "Thanks, Bubbe."

"Do you need help carrying that?" Logan gestured at all my luggage.

"I'll manage." I jerked my chin at his baggage. "You've got more than me."

"Oh." He chuckled. "I guess I do."

In the end, we made it because Dad handled the doors.

"Call us if you need. Remember, you can come home on weeknights this year too, Logan."

"Home?" He blinked.

"Yes." Dad nodded. "If you're not too busy studying, smartypants."

"That's Mr. Smartypants, Dad." I smiled.

"Gotcha." He winked.

With that, we walked through the interior door he'd held open and into the Hawthorn Academy lobby.

"This is...different." Logan stopped in his tracks.

"Do you need a minute? Because I sure do."

The changes were subtle, considering the way everyone else milled around the lobby. However, a person sometimes overwhelmed by his surroundings and a solar magus could not ignore this. The entire lighting system had changed.

"It's awfully harsh." Logan glanced up at the ornate magical chandelier. "Poor Zeke."

"I was going to say the same thing." I sighed. "Last time, it was like an autumn afternoon, but this is desert mirage levels of sunshine here."

"No kidding." Dorian brushed past us on his way through the door at our backs. "Good thing I've got built-in AC." Julia hooted sleepily on his shoulder.

"I'm beige and getting a sunburn," Dylan chimed in while sauntering over from the stairs.

"What's up, Jerk!" Dorian smirked.

"Nothing much, Coward." Dylan rolled his eyes.

I froze, waiting for the inevitable showdown I'd have to stop.

They'd had enough of those last year for me to recognize when one was imminent. But they didn't start fighting. Instead, they did some kind of secret handshake.

"I don't get it," Logan said.

"Different strokes, man." Dorian shrugged. "Anyway, race you to the stairs!"

I got there first but went up a few steps and waited for the others to get on before calling out our floor. The steps moved upward like a magical escalator, which was always nice at the beginning and end of terms when everyone had luggage.

Gale, Dylan's dragonet, did the same nostril-flare at Bubbe's case that Ember made earlier. Then he peered at my hair, looking for her. She'd hidden pretty effectively. He tugged Dylan's ear, chirping.

"He's in a state over that thing. What is it?"

I swallowed and tugged my collar as my face blazed like the stupid chandelier.

"Brooding box." Logan clapped his hands, almost losing the bag draped over his shoulder. "Bubbe thinks Ember might nest this year. Isn't it exciting?"

"Wow." Dylan blinked.

Before we could say more, the stairs stopped, and we had to part ways to get to our rooms. Dorian followed me because the room he shared with Eston was on the way to mine.

"You're worried about Ember mating. Why?"

"I thought maybe she's a little young. And she hasn't ever met any other dragonets."

"Bullshit, Aliyah." He lowered his voice. "With the changes on campus, we should be straight with each other. Well, in a manner of speaking, anyway."

"Can we talk about this somewhere more private than the hallway?"

"Sure."

He dropped his luggage off in his room, told Eston he'd be back in a while, then waited until we were inside my room.

"Go on."

I opened the suitcase with my hanging clothes and started unpacking it so I'd have something to do with my hands.

"I think something's wrong with me." I turned my back, hanging a pair of blazers. "I'm not comfortable. With sex. Like, at all."

"Okay." I turned to find him nodding. "There's nothing wrong with you."

"But, like, everyone else." I glanced at the still-empty bed across the room. "Noah figured out he was gay in middle school. Grace has been all over Az this summer." I closed my eyes. "I don't know anyone like me."

"Maybe you do. We'll get to that in a minute." He sat on Grace's bed, then patted the spot beside him. I hesitated.

You saved his life. Let him help.

I nodded and sat.

"There aren't only hetero, homo, and bisexual people. Some people aren't sexual at all."

"Wait; what?" I blinked. "Like, they never fall in love or what?"

"No. Some fall in love, even get married and have families. But they don't get attracted to other people in a having sex way."

"Not ever?" I blinked.

"I don't know." He shrugged. "Still, you're not alone. Not by a long shot."

"Anyone can be like this? Like, not just us?"

"Absotively." He nodded. "Mundanes and all kinds of extrahumans."

I sighed. "It's a relief, knowing it's not a, um, weird extramagus thing."

I was about to ask him exactly what he meant about me not being alone. Was there someone else, maybe even a person I knew, who felt the same way I did? But the latch clicked, and the door opened, revealing Grace. She held it and let Lune hop inside, then walked in.

"We're all running late. It's almost time for the headmaster's welcome assembly."

"Wait; what?" Dorian pulled out his pocket watch and checked the time. "That's way earlier than last year's."

"Yeah. New headmaster, new rules." Grace set her bags down and jerked her thumb over her shoulder. "It's in five minutes."

We got up and followed her out into the hall.

"Oh, I should warn you about Hiram."

"Do it while we walk."

I gave them the basic gist of Professor Hawkins' explanation.

"This is gonna suck." Dorian sighed. "Oh well. So much for fun this year."

Grace snorted. "If the kid who transferred from The Academy is this worried, we're screwed."

We had no idea until after the assembly how much.

I sat in the front row at the end of the aisle. Grace sat beside me, and Logan directly behind. Dorian sat across the aisle. The clock on the wall behind the empty podium stood at scant seconds to ten in the morning although the lights made it feel like high noon. The squeak of rubber-soled shoes made me turn my head, expecting Dylan, late from a shift at the cafe.

He doesn't work there anymore, remember?

"Can I—"

A *crack* and rush of air interrupted Alex, who stood like a deer in headlights, holding his green apron in one hand. I nudged Grace, and we both scooted over. As Alex was about to take the seat, he vanished in another one of those whooshing *cracks*.

"Mr. Onassis." The voice boomed through the room but was somehow raspy with a slight quaver. "I don't tolerate tardiness. If it happens again, there will be consequences."

Alex stared out at the audience. Yes, the bunch of us felt more like a group watching a staged performance than a gaggle of assorted students at their first day of boarding school, because that's what Hiram Hawkins intended, of course.

Astute. Your new headmaster is, as you say, "old school" and will employ methods your parents are more accustomed to. Consult them, and there's hope for you yet.

I wasn't the only one who noticed, either. It wasn't much of a surprise that the kid from the school for delinquents knew that to do next.

"Sorry, sir," Dorian whispered from across the aisle.

Unbelievably, Alex took his advice. Sort of.

"I'm deeply sorry, Headmaster." He bowed so sharply his jet curls bounced.

"Purchase a timepiece." Hiram Hawkins narrowed his eyes, and Alex vanished again, reappearing at my side in the seat, head over knees.

"Sit up." I elbowed him.

He did.

"For the First-Years, welcome. It's my hope that you'll thrive in the structure I've built since my arrival." The new headmaster grinned. "As for the upperclassmen, you'll have some changes to get used to. First, some faculty arithmetic. Ezekiel Brown is working elsewhere. Nurse Smith will be assisted this year by an Emergency Medical Magus. We have another new addition to staff, Ms. Rupi Khan, our school counselor."

A smattering of applause covered Grace's question.

"Ms.?" She nudged me.

"Divorced. Ask Dylan."

"Additionally, all seven of the trustees on our board will live on campus this year. You'll get the chance to meet them at the mixer this evening. They'll be auditing your classes, so take the chance to get to know them sooner rather than later."

This time, whispers and gasps sounded throughout the lobby.

"However, their quarters in the Faculty Annex are strictly off-limits to students. Likewise, they are restricted from entering your dormitories. Including those who are family members. I demand professional levels of decorum from both the trustees and you students."

"Relief city." Alex leaned back in his seat but shot me an intense glance. "You'd better avoid my mother, Morgenstern."

Easier said than done, but nice of him to warn you, I suppose.

Warn me? I thought.

Yes. I imagine learning to speak Prince of Darkness will be useful this year.

"Finally, I welcome you all to get familiar with the common areas and your roommates.. Dismissed."

He grinned, then vanished with a *smacking* sound.

"That's some seriously strong space magic." Grace shook her head.

"He's the most powerful one on the planet." Alex shook his head. "Watch what you say in here."

"Um, thanks, I guess."

"Look, I'm serious. About him and the woman who birthed me." On his shoulder, Asceco hissed.

"Okay. I hear you. Why the help?"

Before he could answer, Ember screeched and took off from my shoulder. She winged into the air, banking toward Gale, who'd soared by. They circled each other while flying off together into the shadows of the rafters.

I blinked, crossed my legs, then pressed my hand against the middle of my chest where my heart threatened to break ribs.

"You're in for it, Morgenstern." Alex stood and slung his apron over his free shoulder.

"What?" Grace stood and put her hands on her hips. "You did not threaten my friend, Onassis."

"It's a warning. Asceco mated three years ago." Alex shrugged. "Good luck with that."

He sauntered off.

"Oh no." I hung my head, hiding in my hair. However, my tresses couldn't protect me from the implications. My familiar's desires could impact my emotions, no matter what I did.

Hopefully not your actions. Because he slept with Noah's boyfriend back then.

The voice didn't console me, but Grace's hand on my shoulder managed to.

"Don't pay attention to him. Let's go get beverage roulette."

I nodded and followed her into the cafeteria, but once I'd had some food and drink, I couldn't focus on the conversation. Or much of anything else. My face felt flushed and my pulse racy. I excused myself and headed for the infirmary. By the time I made it down the ramp, I practically collapsed into one of the chairs in the waiting area.

"Whoa!" The guy trotting toward me wasn't Nurse Smith. He had curly hair and held a wand, which he used to tap his spectacles, then pointed at my forehead. I didn't notice any hint of a familiar anywhere. "You're running a slight fever. Any other symptoms?"

"Um, my heart."

"Hmm." He pointed the wand at me again. "Yeah, looks elevated. And your blood pressure's high. Let me help you into—"

"Ian, what are you doing?"

"Uh, helping, um, what was your name, Miss?"

"Aliyah." I gasped, my heart fluttering. "Morgenstern."

"I see that, but you haven't checked for her familiar." Nurse Smith glanced around the room, then upward. "Where's Ember?"

I mumbled something about her and Gale going off together.

"This sometimes happens to bonded magi, Ian. You've got a lot to learn about the way that works. Still, it can't hurt to let her rest." Nurse Smith sighed. "Set her up in room one if you think company will help."

"But there's a patient—"

"She's on his list of permitted people."

I wasn't sure what he meant and wasn't in the right mindset to reliably ask without it coming out weird, like when Ian asked my name. So, I let Ian lead me into room one, where I sat on the bed beside Hal's. Ian waved his wand, and the foot elevated.

"To help your blood pressure," he explained.

"You didn't forget to hydrate and collapse again, Aliyah?" Hal asked once Ian had gone.

"No." I turned my head away. "How are you?"

"It's infusion time again." He chuckled. "Dad insists, although I still have mostly good days."

"Is that why Faith's not here?"

"She wanted to help Kitty unpack."

"Cool."

"How'd it go with Logan?"

"Um."

"That bad, huh? Sorry."

"No. It started awkward but ended up good."

"So you're together?" Hal grinned.

"I didn't go there." I stared down at my hands. "I don't want to end up in a situation. With everyone assuming. Again."

"Logan's not Alex. But you're the only one who can figure out what you feel."

"How did you do it?"

He took his time answering. I looked back at him. Hal's skin was bright instead of ashy, and the area under his eyes wasn't puffy like it had been last year. Something about his cheeks, how they'd lost their roundness, bothered me. He might not feel stretched too thin, but Harold Hawkins looked that way to me.

"I read Faith's essay. Like I read everyone's our first year. It told me about her circumstances. The second I laid eyes on her, I knew she was constantly angry, in pain. But underneath it was this strength. I thought, we need her on our side." The corners of his mouth tilted up. "You saw it too."

"Yeah." I nodded. "I knew as soon as school started that Faith needed some real friends. I tried so hard, but nothing worked until you talked to her. What happened?"

"It was that day in the cafeteria before you tangled with Charity. She ran off."

"You went after her."

"Right. Because it was my duty. We talked. And changed each other's lives."

"I mean, I saw some of that. But when did you know? Like, what was going through your head at that exact moment?"

"I held out my hand. She took it, and honest-to-God magic happened. When she let go, it was still there." He sighed and beamed.

"That's one of the most beautiful things I've ever heard, Hal." I shook my head.

"But?"

"There's not really a but here. I wish something like that could happen to me."

"Nobody ever does it the same way."

"For Bubbe, it was like you." I sighed. "Her brother introduced them and instant magic. Figurative on his part. He was mundane."

"Oh." He reached across the space between the two beds and patted my hand. His arms were long enough to do that now. "Your story doesn't have to match your family's. Mine doesn't."

"What do you mean?"

"Grandpa and Grandma had an arranged marriage. Dad chased my mother for months. She was totally afraid of commitment. Faith and I are totally in love since that first day."

"I'm having a hard time figuring out what anything means. Romantically, anyway."

"Well, we have a counselor now. Maybe talk to her?"

"Good point." I nodded. "Any other ideas, though? I mean, in case that doesn't work out."

"Grace."

"Oh."

"What's wrong?"

"I'm not sure we share a, um, perspective."

"Ask her about Azrael sometime."

"I think she'll talk about, uh, sexytimes if I do that. Like Cadence does."

"Hmm." Hal lifted his arm to scratch his head, but the tube connected to it hindered his movement. "What about Izzy?"

"Only for a reading."

He nodded. "Logan himself? I mean, he's one of your best friends. And it's efficient."

"I don't know. He's in a state because his mother's a trustee."

"That entire thing is an accident waiting to happen if you ask me."

"Their wing's off-limits. And our dorms are to them."

"I'm not sure that'll make a difference."

"You think they'll barge in?"

"No. Only that there's ample opportunity for them to interfere with us despite that." He sighed. "Grandpa's rules are hard, but they're limited until someone blatantly violates them."

"That doesn't bode well."

"I'll do my best to head off that kind of crap."

"Are you sure that's safe?" I blinked. "I only mean that you're mostly okay until you conjure. I still want you to survive and have a gaggle of kids someday."

"Conjuring space and moving through it is totally different from keeping tabs on where certain people are. I only have to worry about the three trustees we know are bad actors. No need to track Masters, Gauthier, Thurston, or Dunstable. They mean us no harm."

"Thurston? Like the headmistress at Providence Paranormal?"

"Yeah. He's her dad. The worst he'll do is encourage us to apply there."

"So you're planning to keep tabs on the other three?"

"When class isn't in session. They have to submit forms to Grandpa before auditing classes."

"You still have access to the records with him here?"

"Yes. He's a stickler for the way things have always been. Nepotism is one of those. I'm going to use it to our advantage."

"I'm glad you're on our side, Hal."

"Ditto."

A chime sounded from the wall. Ian and the nurse entered the room, took Hal's vitals, and unhooked him from the tube in the wall. I knew it led into the Under and was a way to funnel raw magic into his system. The medical professionals thought he still needed that, despite his positive attitude.

Hal's not out of the woods, not by a long shot. Be careful.

I nodded but refused to give that idea any more room in my headspace that day. We still had a mixer to attend before we could rest, after all.

For the first time in three years, I got to try the punch. As I sipped from my cup, tasting coconut, cherry, and something like citrus, Alex tiptoed over. He pulled a metal flask from his blazer.

"Um, no." I wagged my finger at him.

"You're not in the shitty parents club, Morgenstern. Don't judge." He sneered at someone behind me. "Goes double for you, Spanos."

"Let her get a refill then," Dorian said behind me.

"Fine."

I ladled enough punch to refill my cup. Then he upended the flask over the bowl. Grace sidled up, stirred, and poured for herself.

"What is this for, exactly?"

"Spiking punch." Alex smirked. "And spiting trustees."

"Cool." Grace raised her glass.

"What about the younger students?" I elbowed her.

"The first-years aren't sticking around after their introductions. Most of us are legal in our own countries. Anyway, loose lips sink ships." Grace glanced toward where Mrs. Pierce sat with Mr. Fairbanks. "I want theirs to go down like the Titanic."

"Sentiments." Alex dipped a fresh cup in, not bothering with the ladle. "Exactly."

"I can't believe the two of you agree."

"Get used to it." Grace sighed. "The dogs of war can't be picky. Besides, Dorian trusts him. At least this far."

"War?"

"You expect peace after last year?" Grace gestured vaguely behind us. "With the enemy on campus like this?"

"No way," Dorian agreed.

"I'd kind of hoped we could have a normal year, yeah." I sighed.

"You can try. I mean, we all could." Dorian shook his head. "But we'd get swallowed up."

I opened my mouth, about to say something, anything, to try and prove them wrong. But the magipsychic screen lit up and the presentation introducing the new students started.

I sipped my punch, standing in the shadows to one side as I watched faculty and other adults come and get their drinks. Alex was right, the three untrustworthy trustees all had multiple servings of spiked punch. They didn't notice, either. I watched Nurse Smith and Coach Pickman spill their drinks into a potted plant near the door.

Professor DeBeer sipped, blinked, then chugged hers. She had five more, too. I wasn't entirely sure what kind of effect that might have on a stressed-out professor who'd seen her colleague dead on the floor less than six months earlier. Tears stung my eyes as I considered it.

Minutes later, she paced from the room, eyes on her feet and hand on one wall, treading unsteadily. Professor Hawkins followed her after glancing over his shoulder long enough to catch me looking.

"Hey, Aliyah. There's someone I want you to meet. My mom."

I turned to find Dylan standing beside a woman who looked a lot like him. Her skin was the same deep beige and her curls twisted in the same ringlets although she hadn't dyed them blue.

"Um, hello." I held out my hand. "I'm Aliyah Morgenstern."

"Dylan's told me so much about you. And your brother, Noah." She clasped my hand. "I wish I could have seen the two of you play Bishop's Row last year."

"Oh." I blinked. "You're a fan?"

"I played first defense for seven entire years between prep and uni." She grinned. "From what Dylan tells me, you have enough talent to go pro."

"That's what I'd say about him." I glanced aside. "I'm decent, but he's the real star."

"Don't sell yourself short," Dylan advised. "Or I'll tell Bubbe."

"Back at you." I smirked. "It's nice to meet you, Mrs. Khan."

"That's Ms. now. Likewise. I'll see you and the rest of your classmates around this year. I'm excited to work with the third-year students. I bet you all have excellent college prospects."

"I guess."

"Aliyah's totally a shoo-in for PPC." Dylan grinned.

"There's a college and career event at the Hawthorne Hotel this weekend for seniors from all the area schools," she said. "They'll have a table."

"I'll mark my calendar." I nodded.

"Oh, Mom, there's Logan!" Dylan pointed. "Sorry, Aliyah, but I've got to introduce them."

I nodded and looked away, letting them monopolize my best friend's attention. It made my escape that much easier. As I ascended the moving stairway alone, I breathed a sigh of relief.

You can't run from Logan forever. Or Bubbe. Or that test coming in October. Or college applications.

"One day at a time for now, imaginary friend."

The voice protested as I made my preparations for bed. Despite the fact that I hadn't fully unpacked, I went to sleep. All night, I dreamed of tests. Thankfully, the type taken at desks and lab benches and not in isolation behind magical glass.

CHAPTER SEVEN

The classroom was the same one we'd sat in with Professor Luciano for almost two years. Part of the difference came from the drawings on the magipsychic screen, done in a different hand and style. Mostly, it was the desk placement.

Instead of rows, Professor Hawkins had our seats arranged in a circle. Dorian sat on my right and Faith on my left, closest to the professor. Hal sat between Logan and Dylan directly across from us. The fact that Faith was basically up front surprised me. Until I realized she was making more of an effort at academics this year than the last two combined.

Normally, Logan was first to raise his hand. This year, Faith preempted him nearly every time. Dorian gave her the side-eye more than a few times. Dylan raised his eyebrow almost every five minutes.

Professor Hawkins took it all in stride. Despite the fact that he'd had us at our normal dynamic at the end of spring last semester, he went with the flow. I couldn't imagine that was good for Logan, whose academic primacy had become something of a routine. When we broke for Creatives, he told me otherwise.

"It's kind of a relief." Logan sketched out a horizon on the canvas with a length of charcoal from his art set. "Faith wrote to me all summer and told me about her plans. She wants to do well enough for a scholarship."

"Aren't you worried?"

"About what?" He reached for a thicker piece of charcoal.

"No longer being valedictorian?"

"I already have a full ride at PPC if I keep it above 3.5 this year." He grinned at my chin. "That's the rest of the news that came with my Hawthorn scholarship. College is the most important thing about grades for me."

"Good point." I smiled back. "Guess I'd better get to work."

"Why?"

"Well, because I always wanted to be—"

"You need to work on something, Miss Morgenstern."

"Yes sir, Professor Hawkins." I nodded. "See you later, Logan."

I wandered around unable to settle on a creative project. Clay was okay but nothing exciting. Woodworking reminded me too much of last year. Grace was teaching Hailey how to sew knits.

"Want to make scented candles?" Kitty gestured at a shelf full of wax and essential oils.

"Hmm. Yeah. That sounds good."

We worked with wax for the rest of the time. Then my class headed off to gym while DeBeer's went to the library. Kitty and I said goodbye. Once inside the gym, I headed directly toward the locker room. Coach Pickman blasted her whistle at me.

"Morgenstern! Front and center!"

"What's up, Coach?"

"You're captain this year for the school's Bishop's Row team."

"What? We haven't had—"

"Tryouts, I know. Those are next Tuesday. You and Khan are on the team already. He's still reverse point."

"Shouldn't he be captain, then?"

"He said if you weren't in charge, he wasn't playing. So, we made a deal."

"Oh. Well, what do I have to do?"

"You'll be at tryouts, with veto power. And running conjuring drills, strategies, and focus exercises every time we practice."

"Is it really that big a deal though? Compared to last year, I mean."

"We're trying to work out a way to play the other schools. Off-campus this time. Colleges are interested."

"Like, with scouts?" I blinked.

"Yeah." She nodded. "Providence Paranormal's starting a national college Bishop's Row team next year. You'd better apply there."

"Wow." I grinned, despite my fear they'd never accept me. "Thanks, Coach."

"Don't thank me yet." She nodded. "Captain's harder than it looks. Keep the off-campus plans secret for the time being. Half the trustees don't like the idea. Now get changed, Morgenstern."

I did, quickly. We ran laps, put on our equipment, and did drills. Hal even participated after showing the coach a note from the nurse. Was he thinking of trying out for the team? Was this what Coach meant about it being hard to captain a team?

You'll find out.

After our drills, Logan spoke with the coach. Right before dismissing us to change and shower, she blew the whistle and waved us toward the bleachers.

"Bishop's Row tryouts are next week on Tuesday afternoon. We'll have cheer squad again this year, too. Those tryouts are the same day."

"Why so early?" Faith blinked.

"Because extra practice makes extra perfect."

"Okay." She nodded.

On the way to Lab, Faith stopped me in the hall.

"Should I bother trying out?"

"That depends." I chewed my bottom lip, trying not to blurt the news to her.

"On?"

"How serious you are about all the academic work."

"It's that obvious?"

"Logan filled me in. What's the deal?"

"I'm applying for Alternative Therapies at PPC."

Of course, she wants to be a doctor. Good on her.

"Yeah." I nodded. "I can see you doing that."

"You're not going to advise against it?"

"No way. Go for it."

"Thanks, Aliyah."

We headed into the lab, where I waved her toward a momentarily confused Logan. They sat together at the bench in front while I partnered with Dorian.

"Team Miscreant?" His grin was too shallow.

"Nah." I gestured at Ember, swooping lazily toward the perch Julia already sat on. "I don't aim to misbehave this year. Let's be Team Airborne."

"Okay." He nodded. "I don't want trouble, either."

This year, there wasn't anything so simple as a lab safety tour. Instead, we got right to our first experiment, one where we had to slow the growth process of a fungus from the Under.

"Usually, I'm the first to say I love a fun guy." Dorian raised an eyebrow, conjuring ice at the bottom of the flask containing the gray mushroom. "But this is ridiculous."

"Ha." I held a hand over the container, thinking of the mid-morning sun in autumn. I didn't want to sauté our specimen, merely inhibit its growth. Overall, we were doing pretty well. Hal and Dylan had chosen a similar tactic, but they had trouble heating their air.

"Wait a minute." Hal glanced at me, then narrowed his eyes.

My inside voice giggled as if someone had goosed it. I blinked and almost dropped my beaker.

Tickles!

I laughed.

"Aliyah?" Dylan stared at the space between my conjuring hand and the top of the beaker. "What just happened?"

"My bad." Hal shrugged. "Just used my space to borrow us a little sunshine."

"Never mind." Dylan shook his head.

I thought that was the end of it, but after Lab, I tried heading to the infirmary to see if any first-years had Familiar Bonding. I wanted to keep track of them in case they needed help. Before I turned the corner toward the ramp down, someone tapped my shoulder. I turned to find Dylan.

"Hey."

"What's up with you?" He scratched his head.

"Huh?" I played dumb. Because I was pretty sure whatever he'd noticed had something to do with the inside voice.

Not him. You're supposed to tell Logan first.

"It just happened again." He narrowed his eyes. "I'm taking you to see my mom."

"Wait, no." I shook my head. "I'm okay."

"Then why is there," he waved a hand at the top of my head. "All this?"

"I don't know what you mean."

Overhead, Gale warbled out a melody. Ember responded by peeping and launching off my shoulder to follow him.

"Is it that?" He jerked a thumb at the dragonets. "Ember going broody and taking Gale with her?"

"I don't know." I shrugged. "Maybe you can explain exactly what it is that's worrying you?"

"Um." This time he blinked. "No. Actually, I can't."

"How about we talk after you figure that out?"

"Okay, I guess." He nodded.

"Let me know when."

We parted, and I headed down the ramp, not bothering to call Ember. I stared down at my feet, sighing. Should I find Logan instead? Or maybe Dylan had a point and I should talk to his mom. We had a school counselor for a reason.

"Whoa!"

I didn't get out of the way in time and ended up on the floor.

"Sorry, Aliyah." Logan stood over me, holding a hand out to help me up. I took it.

"It's okay. I was thinking about you."

"You were?" His mouth dropped open.

"Can we talk?"

"Yeah. Dinner?"

"It's not a public subject. Can we drop my bag off in my room, talk, then get food?"

"Sure."

We walked through the lobby in a tense sort of silence. I was relieved to find my room empty. Doris jumped up on the bed, chirping at the empty headboard, where Ember often perched.

"Where's Ember?" Logan asked.

"Probably with Gale."

Definitely.

I sat, closing my eyes. When I opened them, Logan had stepped back, eyes wide and one hand over his mouth.

"What's wrong?"

"You didn't ask me in here because—" He dropped his hand and cleared his throat. "Um, because of the dragonets?"

"No." I shook my head. "I need to tell you something. Should have done it over the summer. Maybe even last year. I'm sorry."

"All right." He stepped over like the floor was twenty stories off the ground and made of glass. He sat by the foot of the bed, facing the other side of the room.

Just say it.

"Ever since that fire in the lab, I've heard a voice in my head."

"Wait." Logan turned, eyes narrowed. "That's...different."

"You don't think I'm crazy?"

"No way. It's mysterious, though."

"Believe me. I know that feeling." I swallowed, my throat suddenly tight. "I never told anyone before. Professor Luciano—" I sniffled, eyes stinging. "He figured it out." My voice broke, but I continued anyway. "Some extramagus thing. Said he'd teach me about it. But then he—he never got to."

"Oh no." He slid over and pulled my head on to his shoulder. "It's okay."

"It's not." I sobbed. "Everyone will think I'm evil again."

"I don't. You're different. Maybe it's a talent, like mine. We can learn about it."

We rocked back and forth for a while. The motion reminded me of being out on the harbor with Dad, in the outrigger canoe that used to belong to Grandpa. The salt on my cheeks and those sunlit seafaring memories soothed me enough to speak again, finally.

"How?"

"There's got to be research, books the professor studied." He stroked my hair. "If he checked things out, maybe the Ashfords have records."

"I hadn't thought of that." I pulled away enough to look at his face. He'd been crying too. "Not since first year, when I found some articles about extramagi. They didn't have much. Then I forgot to look any further."

"You get distracted sometimes. That's okay." He squared his jaw. "I won't. Consider this my new special interest."

My stomach growled.

"Speaking of distractions." I tried to chuckle, but the sound reminded me of a fish out of water.

"Dinner."

"Yeah." I gestured at my face. "I should clean up a little."

"Me too."

We let go and met up again by the stairs after using the bathrooms. Downstairs in the cafeteria, Dylan joined us but refrained from his earlier line of questioning. Toward the end of the meal, his entire demeanor seemed more relaxed. He smiled an awful lot at Logan, too. When I dropped off my dishes, I turned to see him off in a corner, whispering something to Grace. They giggled but hushed up as I passed by.

I had no idea what they were up to but decided to let it go. Ember was still cavorting with Gale in the rafters. The feelings bleeding through our bond made me hot, cold, giddy, and uneasy all at the same time and I wanted to put some physical distance between us. My dragonet found me in the hall returning from my evening shower. She perched drowsily on my shoulder and fell asleep before my head hit the pillow.

———

The week passed, full of scheduled classes and extra time running in the gym on Tuesday and Thursday. Faith joined me, and I swam with her on Wednesday and Friday. A third person followed. Lena was still as silent as last year but more stoic than shy around us. On Thursday, as we left the gym, we saw Alex beginning a set of laps.

"It's lights out in an hour!" Faith called to him.

He rolled his eyes and ran faster.

"He's trying out?" Lena asked.

"We'll see, I guess." I shrugged. "Are you?"

She nodded.

"Good." Faith nodded.

"Seriously?" Lena blinked.

"Yeah." I winked. "Can't wait to see what you can do on the court."

She blushed, then pushed through the doors to the lobby.

I went home on Saturday morning with Logan, where we both helped out at Bubbe's. Ember sulked all day while Doris kept trying to cuddle up with her. Eventually, my dragonet warmed up to the idea of friend time. They sat on the back porch together and watched a litter of poodles frolic in the yard.

"Will she always be like this?" I sighed.

"They don't mate for life, so probably not," Logan said. "But until any eggs she lays hatch, she'll miss Gale when they're not together."

"At least she'll have her clutch before college. Can you imagine how she'd be if I brought her to some school on the other side of the country?"

"You're not thinking of leaving New England?" Logan blinked.

"I don't want to. But if I can't get in at PPC—"

"You will."

"Please don't say that." I looked away. "In October, after the, you know. Things might be different. I might be—"

"I get it." He rubbed his thumbnails with his index fingers, a precursor to mangling them. "This is your home. You shouldn't have to go so far away."

"It's your home too."

He put his hands flat on the wooden railing. "Not really. Most days, it almost feels like that. I'm mostly like that poor woman in the play that's not really about a streetcar. Depending on the kindness of strangers."

Bubbe called us in then before I got the chance to tell Logan in no uncertain terms that he wasn't a stranger. He was special, important, part of the landscape of my life. At the time, I didn't think I had to put it into words because while working with the animals and relaxing upstairs, we acted otherwise.

Like a family.

CHAPTER EIGHT

The waffle iron was broken so Dad ladled the batter he'd mixed into a hot pan and made flapjacks. Logan insisted on syrup, saying that's the only way he'd eat them. He fed Ember all his strawberries. I spooned his whipped cream into a saucer for Doris, then sat with my now ostentatious looking stack of cakes off the griddle.

"I told you it's odd, topping pancakes with fruit."

"Hmm?"

"Isn't that why you're not eating?" he asked.

"I'm nervous."

"Me too." He nodded. "I'm in, but this is meeting new people. Academics, not showbiz people."

"Is there a big difference?"

"Yeah." He nodded. "Elanor says showbiz has more room for eccentricity."

"You're not meeting professors, though." Mom sat with her plate. "Each school sends seniors or graduate students. They figure you already know about their academic programs. They want you to learn about student life."

"I feel a lot better now." Logan grinned, then attacked his pancakes.

"Me too." I nodded, breaking my fast at a slower pace.

At one point, Logan looked up and smiled at me, syrup smeared across one cheek. My heart felt so full, my eyes stung. At first, I thought my breath caught in my throat too, but unfortunately, that wasn't the case.

You're choking.

I put my hands to my throat. Ember shrieked while rising into the air. Mom dropped her utensils.

Dad was behind me, lifting me out of the chair and attempting abdominal thrusts. Doris stood staring at me, her tail straight up, back arched, all her hair standing on end.

Logan dashed over, kicking my chair out of the way. Finally, Dad got a good grip on me. A burning sensation came with the pressure, but it didn't matter.

A chunk of flapjack flew across the room. Ember batted it with her tail and sent it sailing into the trash. I could breathe again.

"Ow." I winced, clutching my left side. Mom kneeled beside me, as if she could see my ribs through my hand.

"Is it broken, Angie?" Dad peered at her.

"I'm an educator, not a doctor, Aaron."

Logan reached out.

"Can I check?"

I had no idea what he meant, but I nodded because I trusted him. He put his hand on mine, moved it aside, and held it. With the other, he touched the spot that burned and closed his eyes. Doris rubbed her head against his leg, meowing.

"No. It's strained, though." He opened his eyes. "You should take it easy today."

"How do you know?"

"One advantage of being a water magus is that people are mostly water." He glanced at his mercat. "Isn't that right, Doris?"

She purred.

"That's an advanced technique." Dad raised an eyebrow. "Where'd you learn it?"

"Nurse Smith." Logan shrugged. "I asked him to teach me some water-based first aid. After last year, I think it's important."

"I agree." Dad nodded. "Aliyah, do you want me to tape that before the college thing?"

"Nah." I shook my head. "I'll do it myself. Logan's not the only one learning first aid."

I gave up on breakfast after that and went upstairs to change out of my pajamas. Ember followed, staying closer than she had for the past week. I grabbed the tape from the bathroom and washed my face before heading into my room.

Thanks to my reading, I had a good idea of how to tape a strained muscle. However, the book was back on Hawthorn campus. I got my phone and looked it up. While following the diagram I'd found, a message came through.

From Blaine Harcourt, no less. Hoity-toity.

"Hush, you."

"I didn't say—" Logan turned away as I pulled my shirt back down. "Oh. The thing you talked about on campus."

"Yeah. I'm decent. Come in." I held my phone up after he turned around again. "Got a message here."

"What's LORA?"

"An acronym, I forget what it stands for. Blaine asked me some questions last year and put a bunch of information into it. He wants to talk about something at the event today. I guess that means he'll be at the PPC table."

"Makes sense." He glanced up at me. "What's it about, do you think?"

"No idea. Meeting him feels like it happened a million years ago."

"Well then, let's go and find out. Among other things."

"Not in my pajamas, though."

We laughed, and he left the room to let me change.

I hadn't been in the Hawthorne Hotel since that night delivering the letter postponing my extramagus test. I was almost afraid to step inside, but Logan held my hand as we crossed the threshold. The lobby had an entirely different feel in the middle of the afternoon than it had after nine at night. The crowds of students and parents milling around near the ballroom entrance helped, too.

We strolled together along the rows of tables, looking for Providence Paranormal.

"Should have grabbed a program." I jerked my chin at a man reading one.

"It's okay. It's nice to walk."

"Hey!" Cadence flagged us down from a table at the end of that row.

We headed over. She sprang from her seat and hurried around to give us hugs before I got a chance to read the banner hanging from the tablecloth.

"What are you doing working here?"

"Helping my boyfriend's family."

She stepped to one side, posing and making a gesture worthy of a game show hostess featuring a prize. The banner was white with a large black bird emblazoned on it and words below. Logan read them aloud.

"Corvid Couriers: Delivering since 1919." He scratched his head. "You're not a bird. And a delivery company isn't a college."

"Of course not. This is also a career fair and I've got the gift of gab." She winked. "Anyway, they're looking to hire seasonally. And beyond, for an international expansion next year."

"Good luck," Logan said. "Oh no. I didn't mean it that way."

"You usually don't mean any harm." Cadence glanced over her shoulder, then sighed. "But don't let Mrs. Merlini hear you say anything like that. She's a tough customer."

"We'll keep that in mind."

"She's a bitch."

"Mavis!" Cadence blinked slowly and pivoted slightly to reveal the girl behind her. "Language. And honestly, talking about your mother that way isn't ladylike."

"It's true, though." Mavis flipped a lock of jet black hair over one shoulder, looking right at me. "And well-behaved women rarely make history."

"Um, did I miss something here?"

"Your reputation." Logan patted my shoulder. "I think she knows who you are."

I peered at the girl, trying to figure out what was so familiar about her. She might be old enough to go to high school next year, so she'd have been at my grade school if she was local. However, I hadn't met her. Her name gave me the information I needed to place her.

"Hi, I'm Mavis Merlini." She stuck out her hand, which was pale and freckled. "Big fan."

"You must be Crow's sister. I'm Aliyah Morgenstern." I took it. "Do you follow Bishop's Row or something?"

"All of the above." She smiled.

"I don't get it." We shook.

"That's okay." Mavis nodded and let go of my hand. "You're humble."

"She's talking about your heroism, of course." Cadence grinned. "Standing up to someone like Temperance is a big deal in some circles. Even if magi don't make a fuss about it."

"Well, thanks, I guess." I tried to hide in my hair. "Anyway—"

"Look, Aliyah, it's Blaine." Logan pointed across the room. "We're supposed to talk to him. Sorry, but we've got to go."

"See you later, Aliyah," Cadence said.

"Bye." I let Logan drag me away.

"She wasn't kidding about the career part of this." Logan pointed out a table for the Federal Bureau of Extrahumans, where a man with honey-colored hair paced behind a woman with brown curly hair deliberately unfocusing her gaze at passersby. "She seems spacey for a federal agent."

"Probably a psychic, maybe checking auras."

"Look, the Coast Guard." Logan grinned at the purple-haired man behind that table, who had conjured some water into an empty glass.

"Are you interested in some pamphlets?" he asked.

"That depends on three things." I answered. Logan stared at me, mouth open. "Is it the New England Coast Guard? Can we serve either before or after college, and do you have any use for fire magi?"

"We're recruiting for Portsmouth, Salem, Boston, Providence, and Groton. I joined up after college myself but before works too." He ducked under the table to retrieve a box of pamphlets. "We absolutely take fire magi. My commanding officer tells stories about this one guy, a huge hero who was fire and also—" His eyes widened as Ember landed on my shoulder. "Is that your dragonet?"

"Yes."

"This is totally fate." He almost dropped the pamphlets. "Because that guy I mentioned—"

"Must have been my great-uncle Noah Morgenstern." I grinned. "He had a dragonet too."

"Wow!" He chuckled and handed me the glossy folded papers. "Well, look everything over. There's a recruitment bonus that can go toward either tuition or student loans. Plus you get to help people, which is my favorite part."

"Thanks."

As we walked away, Logan asked, "Why the Coast Guard?"

"What you said last night about not going too far away. You were right. If I don't get into PPC right after Hawthorn, I want to be near-by." I cleared my throat. "Near you."

"Really?"

"Yes. Because you're—"

"Ow!" A sharp bark and a series of squeaks followed the exclamation.

"Sorry, Faith." I winced.

She turned, eyes narrowed and gleaming with anger. But they soft-ened almost instantly. Nin and Seth quieted too while peering at me from her oversized tote.

"It's okay, you were busy." She glanced at Logan, then dropped me a wink.

"Um, what—"

"I'm waiting for Hal. He's getting recruited by MIT, I think."

"For that new magitech program?" Logan beamed. "That's amazing!"

"It is." Hal peered over Faith's shoulder. "Last year, I would have stayed on campus and not thought much about the future. It's like life gave me a second chance."

We all smiled at that, but Logan and I excused ourselves because we had to get to the PPC table, which Faith had already visited. Finally, we made it, but Dylan stood in front of it, staring past us at our friends.

"Like a train wreck," he said.

"What's that?" Logan blinked.

"Nothing." Dylan turned his head and dabbed his eyes with a sleeve. I would have thought he'd been about to cry, but then he ran it across his brow, and I wasn't so sure.

Don't fall for that. He's upset.

"We're talking later."

"Yes, we are." He stared at a spot near my right shoulder. Ember was perched on my left, agitatedly looking for Gale. After a moment, he noticed her. "He's outside. Nature called."

"Go on, girl." I gestured toward the door leading outside. She *peeped* and took off. "For now, I'm supposed to talk to Blaine Harcourt."

"Oh, right." Dylan sighed. "Sorry, got in your way, then distracted. Where are you headed, Logan?"

"I don't need to visit any tables." He grinned. "Did you want to take a spin around the room?"

"Sure thing, mate."

"See you, Aliyah!" Logan waved, and they left me standing in front of the table.

"Hi," I said to the burly but friendly-looking fellow on the other side. "I'm looking for—"

"Trogdor!" A short woman I almost hadn't noticed called from the chair beside the man. She had glossy, light brown stick-straight hair held away from her face with a headband.

"No need to holler, Lynn." The big guy pointed across the room. "He's on the way, see?"

"I'm vertically challenged, so no, I don't see." She shrugged, nose still in a book on faerie anatomy. "But I believe you, sleepy bear."

I watched them hold hands, squeezing. It reminded me of something.

You hold hands like that with Logan.

"Let's walk, Aliyah," Blaine said. Then he took off without waiting for my agreement.

"Was that Lynn Frampton?"

"Yeah, my brainiac friend. Yours went off with the British athlete, didn't he?" Blaine strode into the lobby, where the din of a hundred separate conversations couldn't distract us.

"They're roommates."

"Like Bobby and me." He gestured at a pair of tufted chairs near the entrance, then sat in one.

"That's what she meant by sleepy bear? Was he the hibernator? At the beginning of all the, um, trouble at PPC."

"You know an awful lot about my friends." Blaine narrowed his eyes as a puff of smoke rose from his nostrils.

"I mean, said trouble was my blood relative." I sighed and leaned back against the chair, which turned out to be way less comfy than it looked. "Sorry."

"True, and accepted."

"So, what did you message me for?"

"Your test."

"Excuse me?" I stood. "You shouldn't know about that. I don't have to talk about it either."

"You don't, and it was unfair of me to spring that on you. I'm no good at tact. It's part of the fire element. I'm sure you understand."

"Yeah." I sat again. "I get that."

"So. The reason I know about your test started when your uncle called my mother in as peer witness for his extramagus test."

The words that came out of my mouth were ones Faith said last year about her sister. I would have been embarrassed if Blaine hadn't sat there nodding a reaction.

"How dare he?" I finished.

"Somehow, he thought only the *de facto* queen of the dragons could be his peer." Blaine studied his fingernails, then made a dismissive flicking motion. "Anyway, Mother's invited him to all her soirees since then. He went to the latest one and it gave me an opportunity. I might have peeked at the Director-General's schedule."

"You remembered?"

"Kim put all of your information into LORA last year, and it gave me an alert. He's due in Salem on October fifteenth although they don't send letters until the week before. Anyway, we want to help, like we did for Dylan."

"You know what would be better?" I leaned forward.

"Do tell." More smoke streamed out of his mouth with the words.

"Find me a way to record it."

He shook his head. "Can't help with that. You need a memory psychic, and the only one I know is on a job for the next three months at Weir Academy in Niagara Falls."

"Logan knows one." I sighed. "Jacinda Flores. She was at extramurals last year. Everyone swears she's super nice, but it's like she's got a problem with me specifically or something."

"Hmm." He tapped a finger against the arm of the chair, opened his mouth, then closed it while shaking his head. He cleared his throat and spoke again. "You'll have to try harder because the heinous device they use interferes with communication orbs. Even LORA can't record it." He glanced toward the doors leading from the ballroom. "The only way is a memory charm. So you have to make nice with this psychic if—"

Blaine cut his eyes away, focusing on me. He even leaned to one side as though trying to block my view. I narrowed my eyes, frowned, and leaned farther. Which maybe wasn't the best idea.

Logan and Jacinda stood framed by the ballroom doors like a Norman Rockwell painting, him with his hands up and her on tiptoe, leaning in for what could only be a kiss. On the lips.

My hands smoldered against the chair's arms. The light streaming through the glass doors behind me brightened. When Blaine's mouth dropped open, and he stood, I realized it wasn't the sun.

You're going nuclear.

"I'm jealous, okay?"

"It's okay." Blaine nodded, stretching his arms out to the sides. "But I'm not a magus and can't banish your conjures. And burning down historic hotels is not a good look."

"Whoa." Dylan ran toward me from the hallway by the elevator, Ember and Gale flying past him. An icy blast pushed back against my heatwave. "Chill out. What happened?"

The sudden cold shocked my rage. I shook my head because I had no answer. I shouldn't be angry at Jacinda. Logan wasn't my boyfriend. We'd declared our feelings platonic back in first year, and I'd said nothing since.

Dylan's tapping foot practically demanded an answer. Blaine's face creased with concern.

"I need to go cool off I guess." I sighed. "Anyway, that's the memory psychic over there."

I jerked a thumb in Jacinda's direction but didn't dare look. My mind kept conjuring images of them making out in the middle of the lobby.

I wish it would stop, I thought at the inside voice.

Granted.

My mind's eye switched to a memory of Piercing Whispers practicing *Hey Jealousy* by The Gin Blossoms. I snorted.

"Are you sure you're all right?" Blaine asked. "Because I could swear you almost puffed a smoke ring just now."

"I need to cool off. Outside, I think."

"Good idea." Dylan nodded.

"Can you introduce me to that psychic, please?" Blaine nodded.

"For what?" Dylan asked.

"A job. With pay."

"I'll go get her, then."

"Thanks," I said.

Dylan glanced at me one more time before walking away, eyebrow raised. I stared at the floor, hands clenched. I had to go but didn't want to leave without being sure about the memory charm.

"Scram, kid. I've got this."

"What?"

"I know tons about memory charms, including what you'll need in October. If she's got a crush on your boyfriend—" Blaine shook a finger, decapitating my protests on that. "I'm no whelp. I'll handle this. Go bank that furnace."

I did as he asked, stepping outside into the breeze coming off the harbor. Well, indirectly. The Hawthorne Hotel was three blocks inland, but it still got plenty of ocean air when the wind came from the east.

Someone stood against the wall in the shade nearby, but I paid them no mind.

"Morgenstern, you're on fire."

"Go away, Alex."

"No. You're burning for real." He batted at my blazer with one hand, wincing.

"Oh." I waved a hand and banished the embers from my smoldering sleeve. "Guess I need a new one of these."

"I saw you react to something in there. What happened?"

"It was stupid. And not your business."

"Fire safety is everyone's business."

"Afraid I'll burn the place down?"

"Yourself, actually." He gestured at the sooty streaks on my garment.

Dorian walked through the door to my left. He froze and stared, a sheaf of folders and pamphlets in the crook of one arm.

"Like you care."

"I owe—"

"No, you don't. Whatever honor code you're following, I'm not on it."

"Fine." Alex walked past me but turned his head to look me in the eye. "Talk to somebody."

"I will if you leave me alone."

He joined Dorian. I watched them cross the street together, heading back toward campus.

A few minutes later, Faith emerged. She insisted on bringing me back to the Providence Paranormal College table to request an application, singed blazer and all. Bobby said I should expect a package at Bubbe's office by the beginning of October, from Blaine.

As we left, I noticed Logan sitting at a table with Lynn Frampton, going over one of his notebooks. She pointed excitedly at something on the page, and he nodded. He glanced up at us and waved.

The flare of heat in my face and around my hands made me walk even faster, snagging Faith by the arm as she slowed.

"Why'd you ignore Logan?" Faith asked.

"It's weird."

"Try me."

I told her all about Jacinda.

"I'd be angry too."

"Why would you care about who kisses Logan Pierce?"

"Because you do. I'd be jealous if someone up and kissed Hal."

"He's your boyfriend. Logan's only a friend."

"There's no *only* about you two, Aliyah. Maybe in first year, but not anymore."

We walked in silence because I wasn't sure what to say. I'd spent the better part of two years with an enormously uncomfortable crush on Dylan. My feelings for Logan weren't like that at all. I couldn't decipher them beyond my certainty that he was important to me.

"Sorry if that came out bitchy." Faith sighed.

"It's me, not you." I shook my head. "Maybe I'm too confused."

"Okay." She nodded. "If you want to talk about it later, I'm around."

"Thanks, Faith. That means a lot."

I walked her back to campus, then headed back home to pack up my things for the coming week. It'd be busy with tryouts. Maybe the routine of athletics and academics would distract me from this seemingly unsolvable problem.

CHAPTER NINE

Truth Sharper Than Fangs
Noah

The Hawthorne Hotel's ballroom was sun proofed with umbral wards over each of the doors, and I'd used the underground entrance. I stood in the lee of the door anyway, away from the cracks. Unless I'd conjured it myself, any glimpse of sunlight scared me, despite signs clearly marking the wards. If an anti-vamp toe-rag decided to mess with them, I wouldn't know until it was too late.

I waited until Grace DuBois turned around. I caught her eye, gestured at the sign, then the ward. She nodded and gave me a thumbs-up. Being a vampire sucked, but at least I knew an umbral magus I could trust.

Even without any effort toward getting my GED, I'd attended the college and career fair with one fervent hope. That I'd get even one precious glimpse of Jonah Arnold, but he hadn't shown up.

Instead, I witnessed that awful kiss and my sister's anguish over it. She was gone before I could rush to her rescue, and Blaine Harcourt dragged Jacinda away moments later. So I did the next best thing.

"Logan Pierce, how could you?"

"I—what?" He pulled a pack of tissues from his blazer's pocket, got one out, and scrubbed his mouth with it. "What did I do?"

"Oh." I nodded. "I get it now."

"She ambushed me." He wrinkled his nose, curled his lip, and swallowed with a grimace like he'd taken bitter medicine. "I don't get it. All I said was hello."

It sounded more like an assault to me, but I didn't want to traumatize my bestie's kid brother. So I invited him to sit down at an unoccupied table in the corner, away from the doors.

"Are you okay?"

"I don't know. Why did she do that?"

"Maybe she has a crush on you, Logan." I sighed. "But she shouldn't have kissed you without asking first."

"Getting, um, physical freaks me out." He hung his head. "So I'm not gay. Or straight."

"Some people need time and being really close to the right person first. Or to be the one doing the kissing." I patted his hand. "Some people never get into displaying affection."

"Another way I'm built all wrong."

"You're not." I didn't try to look him in the eye although I had some idea what he was going through.

"This can't be normal. I can't be."

"You can be different and still be normal, Logan." I opened my mouth and pointed at my fangs. "All vampy. Still Noah. Same person, only a little different from other people."

"Changing rules is hard."

"Right. But you're not changing. You're discovering. Like a new subject to learn, but about yourself instead of a magipsych lab or history."

"So more like going from dance to cheer?"

"Yeah, something like that." I nodded. "What do you do when you have to study a new topic?"

"I ask a lot of questions and take notes." He rummaged in his satchel. "Oh! I can take notes about this. Like writing down how I feel."

"Exactly."

I watched him set his notebook on the table, take out a pencil, and start writing. Not bullet points or a numbered list, but an academic outline. He wasn't valedictorian for nothing. After a few moments, I realized the project totally absorbed him so I said goodbye, stood, and paced away, hoping to find Jonah eventually.

"Hey." Faith Fairbanks stood in my way.

"Hey?"

"Aliyah's outside. I'm going to see how she is. Do you want me to tell her anything for you?"

"No." Lotan hissed in my ear. "Oh! Remind her to request an application packet from Providence Paranormal. Don't tell her it was my idea."

"Why?" She crossed her arms and looked at me sideways.

"She doesn't always take me seriously."

"Whatever works for you, Noah." Faith shrugged.

"Thanks, Faith."

She waved and sauntered off. I decided to make myself scarce, or better yet, find a decent vantage point to catch Jonah's arrival if he showed up. Even if his lawyer didn't want us talking, I still wanted to see his face. Almost had to.

I worried maybe I'd started to forget him. I couldn't possibly. I loved him, right?

Nobody was at the PPC table when I passed it. When I glanced over my shoulder, I saw the brunette who'd been sitting there earlier chatting with Logan. Not in a flirtatious way, thank goodness. She wore a big sparkly engagement ring and had her notebook out. She seemed to be comparing something in it to Logan's notes. I left them to it and kept walking.

Doctor Elizabeth had been down to see me over the spring. Mostly, she helped me cope with the physical changes. She also educated me about where our powers came from. Vampiric instincts and reflexes weren't designed to help vampires hunt extrahumans or even mundane folk.

Ages ago, our role in extrahuman society was to bring in large and swift game over the long winters or eliminate threats like giant cats or bears. We took blood from our kills in exchange for the meat, bone, and furs. That became the basis for our alliance with the werewolves, whose stamina and resistance to the harsh conditions complemented ours.

Unless we were starved to the point of Rage, a vampire's instincts were to guard our found families against harm.

They didn't teach that in schools like Hawthorn Academy, no matter how progressive a headmaster Hector Hawkins tried to be. Even integrated schools like Providence Paranormal only included that in its more obscure curricula. So it fell to older vampires to remember and pass that knowledge on to whoever would listen.

All of this had a point.

I saw a chair in an alcove with a direct line of sight to the door from the tunnel. As I made my way toward it, a swift movement at the corner of my eye triggered my reflexes and diverted my attention. *Why did I feel predatory in a room full of extrahumans?*

Jacinda walked along the wall that ran parallel to the street. My instincts tracked her as a threat and Logan as family.

Solar magi have bad tempers. Vampires even more so. Experience with one helped manage the other. I strode toward her instead of dashing but ended up cornering her only paces away from the exit to the street. I needed to train my instincts to consider her neutral from now on.

"Jacinda Flores, how could you?"

"I know. I'm horrible."

"That's not—"

"The reaction you expected?" She sighed. "Ditto. Anyway, I'd better go home."

"Don't you still need to check some colleges out?" I blinked. "Or, um, careers?"

"I came for one reason, and he's in the corner recovering from my crap decision."

"Oh."

I watched Jacinda turn as if to leave, but after a few steps, she stopped and looked back over her shoulder.

"What about your colleges and careers?"

"Well, I came here for, uh, a not academic reason too."

"Jonah's not coming. I'm sorry." With that, she continued her trajectory and left through a side exit to the street. Also umbrally warded, thank goodness.

I started a snort that I tried turning into a chuckle. That failed, and it went all the way to a sob. A hand fell on my shoulder, cool but firm. For a moment, I hoped Jacinda had either made a sick joke or lied.

I turned, expecting to look up into the pale, freckled face I wanted to see more than anything else in the entire world. Instead of blue eyes and lips pouty with the fangs behind them, I beheld dark blue curls framing a dusky-skinned and square-jawed face.

"Dylan. Of course, your hands are cold."

"Part of ice magic, I guess." He let go of my shoulder. "Are you okay?"

"I spent most of last year asking you the same question, and now you want to turn this dynamic around?" I raised an eyebrow and sniffed like I meant to quip instead of hiding my heartbreak.

"I mean it, if you don't behave, that's what I'll do, mister." He tried making a stern line with his lips, but they twisted instead into a lopsided grin. "So, which schools are you applying to?"

"None."

"Come on. At least one. Practically every one of these want Bishop's Row players—"

"I won't get in."

"I bet a whole lot of them take GEDs. Especially the nocturnal program ones."

"I don't qualify."

"Wait." He blinked. "You didn't finish?"

"Did the courses, but not the test."

"Why not?"

"Because I don't want a GED, Dylan. I want my Hawthorn diploma. I worked too hard." I swallowed, unable to continue. Why was I saying any of this to him? Because he cared and he was there? He deserved better than me dumping on him. I started to walk away, but he stopped me again.

"Have you tried an appeal?"

"The trustees voted last year against letting me finish, even by distance learning."

"Bollocks." He clenched his jaw, then glanced behind me and waved someone over.

"Hey." Lee waved, joining us along with Hal and Izzy. "What's this about?"

"Getting Noah his diploma from Hawthorn."

"Is that possible though?" Izzy asked.

"There's a new headmaster, so yeah." Hal nodded. "Either once per year or with a leadership change, you can appeal that decision."

"They voted four to three against me the last time." I shook my head. "What makes a new hearing any different when it's still the same board?"

"The trustees are on campus with all of us." Lee grinned. "You know, your friends?"

"Exactly." Hal nodded. "We only have to change one mind. I can figure out which way they voted pretty easily. Dad's not headmaster anymore, but I can still play the family card to get into the office. Give Grandpa the old puppy dog eyes."

Hal's demonstration made almost everyone laugh. I abstained.

"Seriously though, you shouldn't bother." I waved a hand at them as if I could make them all vanish. Or myself, maybe. "It'll never work."

"Let the cards be the judge of that." Izzy patted her bag.

Before I could protest a second time, they practically herded me toward one of the two chairs flanking a cocktail table. I sat and let Izzy shuffle the cards, cutting the deck when prompted. I'd known that drill since she started reading tarot on her seventh birthday.

Nothing could have prepared me for The Wheel of Fortune reversed, right in the middle of my spread. In fact, I couldn't even bring myself to look at the other ones she flipped over because I'd gotten that card in this position exactly one other time in my entire life.

The reading before coming out to, well, everyone. It was the first time I truly took my life into my hands and tried to steer my destiny. If I hadn't, I'd have lived a miserable lie all these years.

"So Noah, these cards say—"

"No need, Iz." I stood.

"Are you sure?" Hal blinked.

"He is." Izzy gazed at the cards, reading them anyway. After a moment, she began to clear them but paused when she came to two Knights, one of swords and the other cups reversed. "Hmm."

"Was it that reversed Wheel of Fortune?" Lee scratched his head. "Has he gotten it before or something?"

"Yes." She nodded. "Tell them what it means, Noah."

"It's time to wrestle with destiny. Unexpected changes are coming for me, and if I sit by, they won't go my way. It's time to do something, try to improve my situation. So if you all are still willing to help—"

The chorus of voices saying yes nearly had me in tears again. But I'm a curmudgeon prone to fits of drama, not a softie. I held them back. A vampire crying is not a good look.

"I trust you guys." I grinned at them, hoping it touched my eyes. "Go ahead and do the thing. Check the decision, sway opinions. I'll write an appeal letter as needed. Just tell me when to send it in."

Dylan seemed relieved. Hal nodded. Lee smiled. Izzy opened her mouth, then closed it again.

The exhibitors had started packing up their tables, which meant this event was pretty much over. Dylan waved goodbye and went to collect Logan, who was still engrossed in his notebook but alone now. Hal trailed after them. Izzy elbowed Lee, who stood aside and turned his back as she approached me.

"What's up?" I asked.

"Those Knights in your reading gave me such a strong vibe, I've got to mention them. But you might not like what they mean."

"I'll put on my big vampire pants."

"I'm serious."

"I know. May bravado be my armor and quips my sword."

"That's what I sometimes call the Rolling Stones formation of suit cards."

"Which is?"

"You can't always get what you want. You already know what Knights signify, Noah."

"Suitors. Of the young and male variety." I sighed, then asked her a stupid question on purpose because I already knew the answer would cut deeply. "Which was reversed again? The Sword Knight?"

"No." She shook her head, reached out, and put a hand on my arm. "Cups. I'm sorry."

"Thanks for being honest anyway." This time, I did dab at the corner of one eye.

"It doesn't mean you should give up, though. Remember that the Wheel of Fortune has the most influence here. Everything's still up to chance and subject to change. The other cards give a difficulty level. Maybe."

"How hard will it be, do you think? Wooing Jonah again, I mean."

"It's going to be brutal. Because I think you have to give Jonah time and space to handle this on his own. Noah, wooing him wasn't in your cards."

"But I can't—" I sighed. "Sorry. You read what's there, so I'm not arguing."

"I wish I'd seen something different, if it helps."

"Thanks for that. See you around."

She linked arms with Lee on her way to the lobby. I headed for the tunnel. As I descended the stairs, my spirits sank even lower. Trust had escaped me since Darren's cheating incident. It wasn't right to judge Jonah's future over my past. But there I was, doing it.

My inability to let go was like my left fang. Something sharp that caused me injury if I wasn't careful. The fang on the other side was impatience, and it had an even keener point.

I'd never been able to wait. So far, I'd been unable to temper it with my new vampiric extended lifetime. It was one reason I never wanted to go into extraveterinary medicine.

Izzy's readings hadn't steered me wrong before. But I couldn't bring myself to accept them.

If I did, it meant that Jonah Arnold wasn't my destiny.

I could try doing everything in my power to prove those cards wrong. But the outlook was not so good.

CHAPTER TEN

Aliyah

Logan said nothing about Jacinda on Monday, and I didn't dare ask. The last thing I wanted was a repeat of my first year when I almost burned the cafeteria down. If I brought it up without figuring out what my problem was, it wouldn't be fair to either of us.

He spent most of his free time at Monday lunch and in Creatives with Dorian, which was typical, although without their notes, which wasn't. I tried joining him and Lee for a to-go dinner in the cafe.

"Oh, Aliyah," Lee twirled his fork in some pasta. "This is important and kind of private. Sorry."

"That's okay." I nodded. "See you guys later."

Logan gazed into his chamomile tea the entire time, only looking up to wave shyly as I left to sit with Faith and Hal.

"What's that about?" she asked. "Are Lee and Izzy okay?"

"I don't know." I shrugged.

"Probably. It's college stuff." Hal added. "Lee's going for early acceptance at four different schools."

"Wow." I blinked.

After that, Ember got a ball out of Faith's bag, and we got

distracted by the adorable game of keep-away she played with Seth and Nin.

On Tuesday, the tryouts usurped every conversation I was involved in, including the one at lunch.

"What if people try out for your team and my squad and we both want them?" Logan finished his grilled cheese sandwich.

"The coaches talk about it and decide what they both want," Dylan said.

"Yeah, compromise is important." I nodded.

"Nobody has to fight over me, anyway." Dorian chuckled. "I'm not going out for either team. Maybe people will stick to one thing."

"I'm going for both." Faith twirled her spoon in the dregs of her soup. "I need whatever I can get on my college applications."

"I hear you," Hal said. "That stuff's important."

"Says the gadgetry genius." Dorian shook his cup. "I'm all out of beverage roulette."

"Bell's about to ring, though."

It did. We managed to pay attention in Lab. Right afterward, I got food to go from Penelope. After a hasty meal, I headed toward the gym to change and do some warmups. The locker room was empty. I stood in the doorway, staring at the arch over the gender-neutral bathrooms, unable to enter.

The yellow tape had been gone since last spring, but my mind's eye supplied plenty of memories about the crime scene, including how it looked before the authorities arrived.

I must have been there for a long time because after the squeak of shoes on wood startled me, my arm had a red mark from leaning in the doorway. I turned around to find my roommate.

"I knew I should have come over here earlier." Grace put her hand on my shoulder. "Are you okay?"

"Not really. There's a lot in my head."

"Let's get changed and run some laps. If you think that'll help?"

"Yeah."

Running occupied my body out on the track, but my mind wandered. Fortunately, away from the life-changing catastrophe last year. However, my thoughts strayed to something still ominous. The almost-overheard conversation between some of the trustees, whose presence on campus hadn't made us miserable yet.

After the third time around the track, I stopped. Grace ran by for a moment but turned and came back.

"What's up? You look like you've seen a ghost."

"I was thinking about last year."

Grace's jaw and shoulder eased as I explained what I meant. She must have been more worried than I thought. Having a target, whether an objective or a person, put Grace in her element.

"I knew we should have followed up on that more." She chewed her lower lip. "Well, we didn't have the opportunity last year like we do now. Maybe they made a mistake, invading campus. Leave it to the umbral magus. I'll find some clues, and we can brainstorm what to do with them. If your parents are okay with some sleepovers, that is."

"Should be fine." I sighed. "But I want you to be extra careful. Hiram's no slouch with the space magic and this is his school now."

"Understood."

A crowd of students came into the gym, heading for the locker room. I didn't bother looking to see who since both tryouts were happening.

Coach Pickman ran Bishop's Row tryouts, and Coach Chen ran cheer squad's. Faith went between both groups as I expected, which must have been taxing. Her main athletic strength was endurance so she managed.

Hailey and Bailey Overton also did dual tryouts. Both of them looked exhausted about halfway through, but Hailey kept her chin up while her twin glared and snapped at everyone.

Grace and Dylan were both brilliant at Bishop's Row, with Lee showing his usual competence. Nothing unexpected there. However, we had a couple of surprises.

Hal tried out. His space magic was nothing to sneeze at and a distinct advantage in the game. I could tell he'd been practicing over the summer, too. Coach Pickman's enthusiastic note-taking during his tryout made me nervous, but she'd given me veto power. If she tried putting Hal on the team, I'd block her. Sure, he'd be disappointed, but both Nurse Smith and Bubbe still seemed too concerned about his health for my comfort.

Lena Zanelli might be the quietest girl at school, but she was practically a force of nature on the court. Her endurance needed work, but she conjured almost as fast as Lee and matched me for speed. She even tagged Dylan out.

"Wow!" Grace clapped. "You're awesome!"

"Thanks," Lena mumbled.

I realized I could make up for vetoing Hal with Lena, no problem. With that all but decided, I relaxed.

Here comes trouble.

"If it's not too late, I'd like to try out."

"Onassis." Coach Pickman blew her whistle. "Morgenstern, swap with Khan! Onassis, there's no time for you to change, but drop the apron and let's see how rusty you are."

He wasn't. In fact, he'd improved since first year—while playing in steel-toed work shoes and cafeteria whites.

"He helps me practice," Lena said to Grace.

He conjured faster than he used to and made a throw I barely dodged. I tossed underhand and almost tagged him, but he smirked and spun out of the way. I burned his next orb with mine, then ran behind him to conjure again. He turned and ducked, so I jumped. It was a fakeout, and he threw high, tagging me squarely in the middle.

Coach blew her whistle, and we stopped. Dylan stood on the sidelines wide-eyed. I crossed to him and passed Alex on the bleachers. Logan stood nearby.

"No cheer squad?"

"Sorry." Alex shrugged. "Got here too late."

The coaches blew their whistles, and everyone headed out besides Logan and me. We sat on the bench together.

"There's no question DuBois is in. The same goes for Zanelli. They'll make our defense amazing."

"That's fair." Coach Chen nodded. "I want both Overtons on cheer squad."

"No problem. I want Fairbanks on second mid. Undeath rounds out Morgenstern's fire and solar to counter vamp and unseelie players from the other schools." Coach Pickman checked her notes. "For reserves, Hawkins and Onassis."

"Veto."

"Who?"

I closed my eyes. Life or death was more important than tolerating a jerk.

"Hal Hawkins." I sighed. "I know he looks better, but I'm not sure he'll be able to keep up."

"Not even with accommodations?" Coach Pickman raised her eyebrow.

"What do you mean?" I blinked. "Does he have a doctor's note or something? Because I think he's got better team synergy than Alex, but I worry. He's my friend."

"I was thinking of leaving him on the bench unless we need an ace up our sleeve. I can replace him with Young."

"I don't know." Coach Chen shook his head. "I'll miss having Fairbanks on squad. I had ideas for Faith's sha and Kitty's sphinx. What do you think, Logan?"

"I think we can use any of the familiars for that idea, except the pigeons. Skinner can do the same tricks, and I want Arick on the squad. He's got the best rhythm out of all the second-years, and he only tried out for cheer."

"What's your opinion on Hawkins then, Pierce?" Coach Pickman asked.

"Aliyah's right. Unless he has a note from his doctor, he shouldn't be doing athletics."

"Hold on." She stood, walked away, and took out her wand. She spoke into it like a phone, which made me even more eager to learn that type of magic in college. If I ever got in.

You will. Somewhere.

"Thanks."

"We both have to do the right thing for Hal, Aliyah. Even if it hurts his feelings."

"Oh." I blinked.

"Was that, um, the thing?" He glanced at Coach Chen, who seemed to be tuning us out.

"Yeah." I nodded.

Coach Pickman returned.

"That was Nurse Smith. He agrees with you on Hawkins." She sighed. "As much as I love an underdog story, you've got your team, Morgenstern."

"Thanks, Coach."

"Chen and I still have to hash things out. Lists post tomorrow morning before breakfast. Dual practice every Tuesday and Thursday. Now scram."

She blew her whistle instead of shooing us away like other faculty.

I headed toward the exit instead of the locker room. Logan looked over his shoulder, then trotted to catch up with me.

"No shower?"

"Upstairs for me." I sighed.

"Oh, right." He nodded. "Me too, then."

We walked together in a silence I hoped wasn't too uncomfortable. I thought I could make my escape and continue avoiding the topic of my bizarre jealousy. He stopped me in front of the stained glass doors.

"Wait a minute." He turned and faced me.

"Okay?" I looked at the mural done in glass. Shadows of other students passing by in the lobby made the shadows on the Unseelie side look like ghosts.

"Aliyah?"

"What?"

I turned my head toward him again and found him impossibly close. Our eyes met, and everything stopped. All the burning rage about Jacinda snuffed itself out, and my worries over Hal faded into evanescence.

"This year, we have three dances. I want you with me at all of them." The corners of his mouth tilted up but his eyes widened almost fearfully. "As my—um."

I blinked.

"Date?" The word seemed to steal all his breath, and he gasped afterward. "Maybe like Lee and Izzy."

"Oh!"

The world seemed to shatter into tiny bits, like the glass beside us must have looked before it got framed up and soldered together. Finally, it resolved into something more cohesive, a pattern of colors and shapes that felt right although I couldn't have described them if my life depended on it.

"But still a date?" I managed. "Because they always say it's not."

"Right. Maybe not exactly like them but—"

"Yes." I nodded as my hands fumbled toward his.

He didn't take my hands. Instead, he caught me up in a hug and lifted me off the floor for a heartbeat before setting me down. I still felt weightless in his arms, the same as every time we'd danced together.

I'm not sure how long we stood hugging like that, but when we broke it off, my eyes were misty. We held hands and pushed through the doors together.

For the first time since starting at Hawthorn, I crossed the lobby without the excruciating awareness of everyone else there and the suspicion they judged my every move. Although people noticed us, it felt different. Like nobody waited for disaster to follow me.

Ember peeped and dove through the air, landing on my shoulder but wrapping her tail around Logan's arm. Doris trotted over and walked between us.

We parted at my door. Grace sat at her desk in her pajamas already. I paced through the room, gathering my shower things.

"Are you humming?" Grace turned in her seat and raised her eyebrows.

"Sorry."

"Don't apologize. You're glowing in a non-fire kind of way. What happened?"

"I'm giving things a shot with Logan."

"Get out!" She jumped up, knocking her homework helter-skelter across her desk. Lune hopped and capered all over the room. "No, I mean don't like, literally get out. Leaping Luna, this is awesome!"

"It is?"

"Wait. Are you happy about it?"

"Yes." I nodded. "Why are you so excited?"

"I know it's a little weird to ship real-life people, but I always hoped you two would get together." She squealed. "Can we hug?"

"I'm still kinda sweaty from tryouts but okay."

We hugged. Grace wrinkled her nose.

"Yeah, you're stinky. Go shower. I'm so excited!"

I headed out and down the hall while chuckling. Life would be a million times harder without the people I cared about in it. They made it better, interesting. Weird too, sometimes.

How else do you learn?

"Right," I said into the empty bathroom.

I regretted having missed Faith and wondered how her reaction might have differed from Grace's. There'd be plenty of time to chat with my friends in the morning. I took my shower and went to bed, more tired than I'd realized.

Before breakfast, I headed to the gym to see the teams. Hal was already there and when I approached he turned toward me, glaring.

"I can't believe Dylan did this to me." His nostrils flared, and his cheeks deepened in color.

"Did what?" I blinked.

"He's reverse point, so he's captain. Must have used his veto to keep me off the team."

"No, Hal."

"There's no other way I didn't make it." His hands balled into fists.

"I'm captain." I sighed. "It's not Dylan's fault."

"*You* wouldn't." He blinked, eyes wide and edged with impending tears. "You *didn't.*"

"I did. Your health—"

"Fuck my health!" Hal briefly flickered like he'd lost control of his space magic. "This was my shot. The only way I'll leave a mark on this school. Maybe even the world."

"That's not true. Hal, you can still—"

"No." He crossed his arms over his chest. "You *know* I'm dying. This is the last good spell I'll ever get. You took this from me. *You*, of all people!"

"I backed her up." Logan stepped between us. "Because she's right."

"You don't know any better."

Logan swayed back, face red as if Hal had slapped him. The air around us grew heavy with moisture. Hal uncrossed his arms and put his dukes up, fists flickering, this time on purpose.

A *pop* and a rush of drier air blew us all backward as Headmaster Hiram appeared out of nowhere.

"No fighting on campus." The water coalescing around Logan's hands vanished, and Hal's fists stabilized. "Even my grandson must follow the rules. If you insist on settling your differences physically, you may opt for a faculty-mediated duel at an appointed time as per the student handbook."

"That's not needed, Headmaster." Logan hung his head. "I'm sorry, Hal. I don't want to waste our third year as enemies."

"Me too," I said. "I'm sorry."

"Harold?" Hiram raised his eyebrow.

"I'm going to see Ms. Khan." He turned and stalked away but paused and turned his head. "I'll decide about dueling later."

We stood together in mortified silence and watched him go. Once the door closed behind him, the headmaster vanished again. Logan put his arms around me.

You've got an awful lot to think about.

I told him what the voice said.

"Me too, Aliyah." He patted my back. "Maybe together. Can I come with you on Yom Kippur?"

"You're not Jewish." I sniffled.

"Is that not okay?"

"It's okay if you want to." I pulled back and studied his face. "We can bring people. Check with Bubbe first."

"I do." He nodded. "I will."

"Are you all right, Logan? What Hal said—"

"I didn't expect it, and yeah, it hurt. But we hurt him too when he literally trusted us with his life. Can we go to breakfast now?"

We held hands all the way to the cafeteria, in an entirely different mood from the night before. We'd both made a horrible mistake, but we could try to make up for it together.

That opportunity didn't come until after Yom Kippur.

CHAPTER ELEVEN

"I can't believe they tried to vote down the town's Bishop's Row tournament!" Dylan slapped a hand on the table, almost overturning my juice.

"Failed, though." Lee sprinkled salt on his eggs.

"Thank the gods." Alex held out a carafe. "Coffee?"

"Um, they never made me do that." Dylan blinked. "Pour tableside, I mean."

"That was under Hector. This is Hiram's school now so you get beverage service." He shrugged.

"I'll have some, thanks." Grace held her cup out.

"So it goes." Alex sighed as he poured.

"Vonnegut rocks," Dorian said.

"You got that reference?" Alex raised an eyebrow while withdrawing the carafe.

"He's my favorite." Dorian grinned.

"Thanks." Grace raised an eyebrow. "Aren't you going to give your fellow fanboy a refill?"

"If he wants."

"Nah. Breakfast beverage roulette is a rare and special animal."

Dorian stood and waggled his empty cup. "I'm hunting it. Come on, Aliyah."

"Um, okay?"

I had no idea why Dorian wanted my company but obliging him couldn't hurt. He elbowed me as we walked toward the section with the cereal, toaster, and drink dispensers.

"So. You and Logan are leaving campus early together?"

"For Yom Kippur."

"He's not Jewish."

"Doesn't matter."

"That's cool." He held his cup under the apple juice dispenser for a moment, then switched to orange. "How are you? With him?"

"Platonic. We talked. When he mentioned Izzy and Lee, it completely changed...well, everything."

"Hmm." Dorian added cranberry juice, sloshed some of his overflowing blended juice down the drain, then added grape.

"Hmm?" I got water because I fasted from Rosh Hashanah to Yom Kippur.

"Our, um, talk on the first day ended kind of abruptly."

"Ah." I grinned and sipped my water as he added a little more apple juice. "I'm still sorting myself out. The plan includes talking to Noah later."

"Good call." Dorian turned his head and met my eyes. "Remember when I said you're not alone if you're asex—"

"Miss Morgenstern." Mrs. Pierce strutted toward us, eyes on me.

"Mrs. Pierce." I resisted the urge to curtsy.

"Happy Yom Kippur." She cradled her teacup in both hands.

"Um."

This holiday isn't happy, and she knows it. Call her bluff.

I didn't.

"Thanks?" I blinked.

Julia hooted and ruffled her feathers while glaring balefully at Logan's mother.

"No." Dorian shook his head. "You don't get to swing your privilege and insult my friend." He put his hands on his hips.

"Excuse me?" She raised her head and looked down her nose at him.

"It's a solemn holiday," he retorted. "Self-reflection time."

"Is this true, Miss Morgenstern?"

"Yes, ma'am."

You gave her an inch. Keep your eye on her, or she'll take a million miles.

"Well, then. May you have a meaningful day." She turned and clicked away on high-heeled shoes, her bouffant bleached blond hairdo not even bobbing as she went.

"Dylan says she reminds him of Margaret Thatcher." Dorian snorted. "Let's get back."

We went to the table. Grace was gone by then, and Logan sat in her place with only a glass of water in front of him. I blinked, wondering why he'd bothered with fasting.

"When in the High Holy Days, do as the Jewish do." He grinned.

"Okay." I sat beside him.

Lee chewed extra crispy toast and grinned. Dylan followed suit with his third breakfast sandwich. Ember took off, launching from the back of the booth to meet Gale, who'd shown up late again. As they cavorted in midair, Dylan glanced across the table at Dorian, who seemed oblivious.

Although I'd leave after lunch, it seemed like this would be a long day.

I left with Logan as soon as Creatives ended. He said he saw no point in sticking around with glasses of water while everyone else ate lunch and I agreed. Ember soared into the late summer air. I almost ran into the Polaroid cart. Azrael wasn't driving it this time, though.

"Um, hi?" I peered around to look at the person on the bicycle end of the contraption.

"Hello!" Mr. Ambersmith smiled. "Let's capture this moment."

He held up one of the cameras. Before he snapped a picture, Logan held my hand. Fortunately, there was no flash. He hated those.

"On the house." Mr. Ambersmith handed Logan the piece of plastic the camera produced.

"Thanks," I said.

We walked along Essex street as the balmy air developed the picture. Logan peered down at it.

"Wow. That's an amazing smile. Too bad mine looks like cardboard."

I snatched the photo from him and had a look.

"I think it's perfect."

Logan squeezed my hand. We continued quietly but comfortably. Logan went directly to Bubbe's as I headed upstairs.

All the curtains were drawn inside the house because Noah had shown up the night before. He hung around the kitchen, sipping from a cup of blood, and helping Dad with the baking. As soon as we arrived, Mom came out of her office and chatted reassuringly with Logan, who was concerned about being dressed appropriately.

"I remember Angie's first time. It was our third year, too," Dad mused as he pressed dough between his fingers.

"Really?" I blinked.

"Oh, come on." Noah rolled his eyes. "Don't tell me you didn't know Mom converted?"

I shuffled my feet.

"With a name like Hopewell? Really?"

"Shh," Dad said. "She doesn't talk much about it, but yes, that's what happened."

"After you started dating?" I asked.

"Pretty much." Dad's smile was faint but genuine. "She officially started the process of joining this family after graduation." He shrugged, his smile now in full bloom. "Unofficially, it started the first time she visited."

"So romantic." Noah sprinkled the last of the flour over the lump of dough.

"Last year, you would have rolled your eyes." Dad chuckled.

"Sorry." Noah sighed. "I got better."

"Can we talk?" I nudged my brother.

"I can handle kneading this for the next fifteen minutes," Dad said.

Noah followed me upstairs but shook his head when I reached for the door to my room. He opened his and waved me inside, where the windows were sun proofed.

"Sorry about that." I sighed.

"Last time we talked in here, this was hot cocoa." He held up his mug of blood, downed the dregs, then set it aside. "The only thing certain in this world is that everything changes. Anyway."

"I'm sorry—" We both said at the same time.

"Jinx. You owe me O negative."

We laughed.

"Seriously." He smirked. "What's up?"

I told him about my conversation with Dorian on the first day back at school.

"So, I did some searches on days off-campus. Do you think I'm asexual, Noah?"

"Maybe." He sighed. "At the end of the day, all you can know is how you feel and what you want."

"Well, I don't want sex. Love? Yes, please."

"Unsurprising." He grinned gently.

"How?"

"The look on your face every time Cadence talks about cute boys. Or Elanor about pretty girls." He took my hand. "Their opinions aren't relevant. Logan's are. What does he want?"

"A relationship. Something like Lee and Izzy, he says." I sighed. "Which made more sense to me than anything else I've seen, but it worries me."

"About?"

"Whether it's love. How do you know?"

"Imagine your life without him in it."

"That's awful."

"Okay, now imagine the world without him. Would you give up the first to stop the second?"

"God, Noah." I closed my eyes, tears running down my cheeks. "That's horrible either way, but I'd do it in a heartbeat."

"You love him, then." He handed me a tissue. "I know this firsthand."

"What about being in love?" I wiped my face. "And his feelings."

"You have to have a serious talk with Logan about that last part. I don't know about the other." He sighed. "For me, love's all tangled up with sex. Maybe you should talk to Bubbe about that."

"Bubbe?" I blinked. "She had Dad. So—"

"She wasn't totally celibate because she wanted a child." He took the tissue and tossed it into the wastebasket by his bed. "When I came out, she said a few things... Talk to her. I mean it."

"Yes, sir." I gave him the weakest salute ever.

"Are you okay now?"

"There's one more thing."

I told him about Hal.

"Oh, no." Noah's eyes widened. "You apologized, though."

"Maybe that's not enough."

"I've gripped grudges enough to know one thing, Aliyah." Noah chuckled but dabbed the corner of his eye. "It's up to the holder to let them go. I pray he finds peace."

"Me, too."

Dad called from downstairs. We headed downstairs and out.

***

Logan sat between Bubbe and me at the service. At first, I thought he meant to be a buffer. I'd felt more distant from my grandmother since June than at any other time in my life. After the first few minutes, it became clear that this wasn't about her or me. It was for Logan.

He took all his cues from her, nodding and following along like he was on a dance floor instead of inside an unfamiliar temple. Although he clutched a weathered old stenographer's notebook, she must have described everything ahead of time, too.

Mom saw me glance at the notebook.

"I used it," she murmured. "Years ago."

When the Shofar blew, I closed my eyes. In my mind's eye, I saw

Filberto Luciano sitting here between Great Uncle Noah and Bubbe in grade school. That scene faded, replaced by what I thought were Noah and me. However, my hair was too short and permed, and Noah wouldn't ever wear acid wash jeans. I realized it was Bubbe again, this time with my grandfather. It was impossible for magi to be psychic, but those visions felt real.

Coincidence is a series of patterns woven by the magic we use. Of course, they are.

When I opened my eyes, Logan was touching my cheek. He wiped away a tear there. When he lowered it, I reached out and twined my fingers with his. I knew immediately that Bubbe and Grandpa went through similar motions decades ago.

On the way out, we walked together behind everyone else.

"You should talk to her after dinner. Bubbe, I mean."

"I will." I squeezed his hand. "What about you?"

"Your mom asked me for my study guides from the first two years."

"Makes sense."

"It does?"

"I bet she thinks they'll help students in the future."

"If that's the case, I'll give her the one from this year, too. Once it's finished."

"You're amazing, Logan Pierce."

He blushed as we got in the car.

At dinner, Logan tried a little of everything, which surprised me. He'd always been a picky eater at school. That trait followed him to a degree because he made a face after sampling the whitefish salad and only took second helpings of challah and noodle kugel. Noah beamed.

"If you ever want me to make that for you, let me know." He jerked a thumb at the half-empty casserole dish, then refilled his cup with blood from the refrigerator. "Vicarious eating isn't the same, but I'll take it."

"Thanks, Noah."

The rest of us practically pigged out. The fast before Yom Kippur was the longest one we observed. Eventually, we all sat back and patted full bellies. After coffee, Bubbe headed downstairs. I waved to

Logan as he got his notes out for Mom, then I followed my grandmother.

"Bissel." She turned, standing in the hall to face me.

"Bubbe." I sighed. "Can we talk?"

"I need to make my rounds, but yes." She raised an eyebrow. "Is this a topic for working or teatime?"

"Maybe both."

"Then start with the part you can manage while we work."

Love or fear. Choose wisely.

"How did you know you loved Grandpa?"

"I'm a serious person by nature, like you, Aliyah. I spent a lot of time worrying. He let me share my burdens. That's how it started."

"So it wasn't right when you met, like how Dad tells it?"

"That only happens in movies and to people like your father, who lean into the physical side of things." She chuckled while refilling a water dish for a sleeping fox. "My first meeting with Morris was a little awkward."

"How?"

"He told me he liked my shirt. Which was covered with fewmets at the time."

I put my hand over my mouth to stifle my giggle until we reached the next room, where a wood owl roosted. He was awake, of course.

"Hoo?"

"Just me." Bubbe grinned at the bird, then swept the pellet it had regurgitated into the dustbin.

This time, we laughed together, but she put a finger to her lips as we approached the final overnight guest. A puffin nested in a box on the floor, beak under her wing.

"Wait." I blinked. "That bird looks familiar."

"Oona's with one of the trustees. He thinks she strained a leg."

"He mentioned that while auditing our lab yesterday." I sighed. "He was nice, but I forget his name."

"Justin Glen from New Hampshire, a family friend of your classmate Eston." Bubbe refilled the small plastic temporary pool with water. "That's his familiar."

"Are all three of them—"

"Shh." She led me back into the hallway. "Yes, the fox and the owl are companions to trustees as well."

"They're all injured?"

"Not that I could tell. Only Oona. But their magi wanted them seen as a matter of routine."

As Bubbe led me toward the kitchen, I checked the doors. The owl's name was Smokey, and the fox was called Zephyr. I'd have to ask around at school, find out more about their magi. Logan would help. I gasped.

Burden sharing, table for two.

Bubbe set the kettle on the stove while I got mugs and tea out of the cupboard. Once we sat with cups steaming in front of us, I drew a deep breath, inhaling the herbal aromas.

"I'll go first," Bubbe said. "I'm sorry for trying to make the choice about your testing for you."

"Why?" I stared at her hands, how only the fingertips touched the ceramic. "You were as adamant as, well, adamantine."

"They called me that in high school." She sighed. "Shiny, but hardheaded. And hearted."

"How?" I blinked. "You're a caregiver."

"It's no easy thing to be, especially for animals, who can't speak for themselves. I choose for them, most of the time. Sometimes, that means wearing armor around my heart. Like I tried doing with you last fall and this summer, although you were willing and able to tell me what you wanted and needed for yourself."

"Wow. I thought you'd been angry with me all this time for going to Rockport behind your back."

"I was, but only for a moment and unfairly." She reached across the table. "Can you forgive me?"

"This isn't what I expected." I took her hands. "Yes."

"Thank you."

"I'm afraid, Bubbe." I looked down at our hands, joined together in the middle of the table. "Of the test."

"That's natural."

"Not normal?"

"Nothing about the way extramagi get treated is normal. Who's your witness?"

"Logan."

"Good." She nodded. "I wonder why you chose him."

"He offered the moment he found out about it." I glanced up at her face. "I realized he would have been my first choice anyway."

"Ah." She let go of my hands, reached for her tea, and sipped. "Will you be afraid still, with him there?"

"Yes." I nodded. "Because the test doesn't make me fear for my physical safety."

"You worry that taking it damages mental health."

"Everything went sideways for Dylan after his. Do you know he almost went home with Temperance last year over winter break?" I shuddered while gazing into my tea. "Then there's Richard."

"Richard's childhood environment was more toxic than a nest of basilisks. He hid what he was for decades and avoided the test until he got arrested. Neither of them had the kind of help and support you do."

"He should have asked someone else to be his witness."

"The school should have had a counselor besides the headmaster." She sipped her tea again. "But running that school's not my business."

"You think I'll be okay, then?"

"If you do the work on self-care before and after, yes."

"What work, exactly?"

"Start seeing Ms. Khan now, and make it regularly. Talk to Logan about what you fear and what he can expect. Then afterward, take time and small steps. With help, from them and your other friends and family."

"I'm not supposed to talk about it though."

"You've got a lot of people who care about you, Aliyah. Most of them are brilliant. I think you'll figure out how."

"Especially Logan."

"You two are exceptionally close since last spring. Is this why you asked me about your grandpa?"

"Partly. Noah had something to do with it too."

"Oh?"

"I tried talking to him about love. We think maybe we're too different when it comes to that."

She raised an eyebrow.

"There's no, um, sex in it for me." I winced. "He said he thought you might understand better than him."

"He's right." Bubbe nodded. "It's never been about pretty faces for me. Maybe I'm not wired like the majority of people. There's no shame in that. I experience love a little differently; that's all."

"So what did that mean for you and Grandpa?"

"When we were together, the world felt kinder. Friendlier. A more joyful place. Does Logan make you happy?"

"Not all the time, no." I sighed. "There's been too much misery going around, stuff not our fault."

"Then what's it like when you're unhappy together?"

"We've done an awful lot of crying on each other's shoulders. Over his parents. The test. Professor Luciano."

"Would those times have been harder if you'd cried alone? Or with a different person, even?"

"Absolutely." I looked up. "Bubbe. Crying with Logan is almost like crying with one of you. Like he's part of the family but not another brother. Is that love?"

"I think you're well on the way to an answer." She nodded. "It's your decision, what your feelings mean."

As we finished our tea, Logan came downstairs yawning. Bubbe cleaned up the tea things, leaving him to walk me to the stairs. Although I had a potential name for the place he held in my heart, I didn't dare say it aloud until I was sure.

The story continues with book Eight, *Speaking with Care*, coming soon to Amazon and Kindle Unlimited

GLOSSARY

People

- **Changeling**- A mortal child of either one or two faerie parents. Most changelings choose a monarch sometime in their twenties, although some do it earlier than they have to.
- **Dampyr**- The mortal offspring of two vampires. They aren't as rare as many suspect, although because their blood is exceptionally sustaining to vampires, they keep their status secret. Dampyr sometimes have magic or psychic powers that work unreliably.
- **Faerie**- A term used to describe either a changeling who has tithed to a monarch and spent a year and a day in the Under or the pure creatures such as Gnomes and Pixies who were created by the king and queen.
- **Ghost**- A dead person with unfinished business becomes a ghost. If a mortal makes a contract before death, that gives them unfinished business and lets them linger. When ghosts finish their business, they move on, but no one knows where they go from here.
- **Magus**- A mortal who can use magic. Magic comes from

energy in the world. Most magi can only use one type of magic. However, a rare few can do more than one kind. Those are called extramagi.

- **Merfolk**- People who can live on land with legs or in the sea with fins and tails. They only emerged from the ocean after the Big Reveal and are still extremely rare outside of harbor towns.
- **Psychic**- A mortal with psychic power. Psychic ability comes from a person's own body and mind.
- **Vampire**- An unliving person who drinks blood to survive and enhance their abilities. Only regular mortals, psychics, and magi can get turned into vampires. Shifters, changelings, and faeries won't turn, and most of those won't survive an attempt.
- **Shifter**- A mortal who can take an animal's shape. Shifters have one form, with coloring similar to what they have while human. They usually have an enhanced sense while human-shaped, which goes along with their animal. For example, an owl shifter might have keen eyesight and a wolf shifter, a great sense of smell.

Shifter Varieties

- **Dragon**- The only shifters who can see both magic and psychic abilities, though only while shifted. The most powerful ones can partially shapeshift. Dragons are immortal and reproduce infrequently. There are so few of them since the Reveal that they've started taking other magical shifters as mates.
- **Kelpie**- A magical shifter who gets their abilities from an enchanted faerie pelt that bonds with their soul. The Kelpie pelts were created by the Goblin King, so they have Unseelie energy and restrictions. A Kelpie's animal form is a horse. Families pass the pelts down through generations,

and part of each ancestor lives on to help their descendants. The ancestors can get distracting, however.

- **Selkie**- A magical shifter who gets their abilities from an enchanted faerie pelt that bonds with their soul. The Selkie pelts were created by the Sidhe queen, so they have Seelie energy and restrictions. A Selkie's animal form is a seal or sometimes a sea otter. They can use water magic as long as they wear the pelt. Families pass the pelts down through the generations, and part of each ancestor lives on to help their descendants. The ancestors can get distracting, however.
- **Tanuki**- A magical shifter with enhanced speed and the ability to see all types of magic while shifted. They are also the only creatures who can manipulate luck, causing it to turn from good to bad or the other way around. They stop aging if they own a charm infused with luck from humans. Very few of those charms exist, having been either used up during the Reveal or locked away.

Powers

- **Air magic**- The power to conjure, control, and banish wind or air.
- **Earth magic**- The power to conjure, control, and banish earth, sand, or rock.
- **Empathy**- A psychic power to sense and influence emotions in other people.
- **Fire magic**- The power to conjure, control, and banish flames.
- **Ice magic**- The power to conjure, control, and banish ice.
- **Lightning magic**- The power to conjure, control, and banish lightning.
- **Poison magic**- The power to conjure, control, and banish poison. Each magus has a slightly different type of toxin they produce. Some are even antidotes to others.
- **Precognitive**- A psychic power to foretell future events.

- **Spectral magic**- the power to conjure, control, and banish light.
- **Spectral Affinity**- A trait some spectral magi have that makes them charismatic and believable.
- **Summoner**- A psychic power that lets the user make contracts with pure faeries, letting the summoner call them in times of need. Each creature has an anchor, some item symbolizing the bond. Mastery of summoning takes decades of study, which is why the most powerful are either vampires or past middle age.
- **Seelie**- The Sidhe queen's court. The Seelie way is about following the letter of the law, even when it's hard or cruel. They have a hard time reconciling faerie rules with the new mortal laws since the Big Reveal.
- **Solar Magic**- The power to conjure, control, or banish sunlight. Some of the most powerful practitioners can find hidden objects or discover long-kept secrets.
- **Solar Affinity**- A trait some solar magi have that makes them beacons for coincidence.
- **Space magic**- The power to move the self or objects instantly across distances. Some can even move other people.
- **Space Affinity**- This space power comes with an ability to locate people or things important to the magus.
- **Telekinesis**- A psychic power that moves objects.
- **Telepathy**- A psychic power to read minds.
- **Tithe**- The process of pledging to either the queen or king, making a changeling choose to be either Seelie or Unseelie.
- **Umbral magic**- The power to conjure, control, and banish shadows and veil or camouflage objects or people.
- **Umbral Affinity**- A trait some umbral magi have that makes them difficult to remember without psychic ability, faerie magic, or a shifter pack bond.
- **Undeath magic**- The power to conjure, control, and banish unliving energy.

- **Unseelie**- The Goblin king's court. The Unseelies bend the rules and often navigate mortal society more easily than their Seelie counterparts.
- **Water magic**- The power to conjure, banish, and control water.
- **Wood magic**- The power to conjure, banish, and control wood. It takes extreme power to influencing a living plant.

Creatures

- **Basilisk**- A venomous serpent that also has poison magic.
- **Dragonet**- A tiny dragon-like creature, always associated with one or more element which powers their breath attacks later in life. They have scales but are warm-blooded like birds. Most don't get much bigger than a small cat.
- **Familiar**- A magical or mythical creature who makes a bond with a magus.
- **Gryphon**- A chimera which has the head of a bird and hindquarters of a predatory mammal. They come in several combinations of base species, and habitat influences their choice in magi to bond with.
- **Karkus**- A crab that can change its shape. They're said to be the offspring of the crab that pinched Hercules as he battled the Hydra.
- **Lightning Bird**- A familiar from South Africa with an affinity for lightning. Its beak can jump-start a car.
- **Mercat**- A shapeshifting feline with fur for land and scales in the water. They can live in lakes, rivers, or in the sea as well as on land. They must never completely dry out, or they will die.
- **Moon Hare**- A magical rabbit that gets power from its particular moon phase. They commonly bond with umbral magi.
- **Pharaoh's Rat**- These natural predators of dragon shifters are the size of ferrets and resemble a mongoose with more

fur. They have an affinity for space magic and can use it on occasion.

- **Pigeon**- Not as mundane as most think, some pigeons have an uncanny sense of direction due to their affinity for air magic.
- **Pricus**- An aquatic goat said to be descended from Capricorn. They can warp time even better than Gnomes.
- **Pure Faeries**- Creatures who spring to life from magical sources in the Under. They are genderless, and their type and ability depend on place of origin. They're associated with only one court, although they will work together to defeat a common enemy.
- **Sand Cat**- A feline that lives in the desert, able to go for weeks without water. Earth magic lets them do this.
- **Sha**- A magical desert dog from Egypt. Sha are the size of mundane toy breeds with short hair and small pointy ears. They could pass for mundane except for their blue tongues. They are attracted to anything undead.
- **Sphinx**- A magic cat with an affinity for fire. The reason they're hairless is that they're resistant to flames.
- **Strix**- A venomous owl with an affinity for poison. Female striges have rounded tufts on their heads, while males have pointed ones.
- **Sumxu**- A lop-eared cat found only in northern China. They are masters of camouflage and have an affinity for several kinds of magic.

Places

- **The Academy**—Something between a community college and a military academy for extrahumans, the Academy is geared toward helping extrahumans who don't play well with mortals get ready to join a blended society. It's got divisions for learners of all ages, though they are housed separately.

- **Cherry Blossom School**- A dojo geared toward teaching extrahumans self-restraint, meditation, and how to temper their enhanced physical abilities with more mundane skills. It's been around for close to a hundred years, run by the Ichiro family. Mundane classes used to be offered as a front but now are a separate division.
- **Ellicot City Magitechnic**- A prep school for magi and psychics specializing in magipsychic technology. It's located outside Baltimore.
- **Gallows Hill School**- Traditionally for shifters, this prep school in Salem recently opened its doors to changelings and other extrahumans not categorized as magi or psychics.
- **Hawthorn Academy**- A preparatory school for magi in Salem. Its campus is in the space between the mortal realm and the Under, giving it unrivaled privacy. They specialize in teaching familiar magic.
- **Providence Paranormal College**- A school founded just one year after Brown University and located right in its shadow. Providence Paranormal used to admit only magi and psychics, but it's been accepting all types of extrahumans ever since Henrietta Thurston became headmistress. There has been trouble since then for students and faculty, leading people to believe dissenters are sabotaging the school.
- **Trout Academy**- A prestigious preparatory school for changelings with magic, recently open to magi and magical shifters. Its campus is located in South County and has been operating in some form or another since Rhode Island Colony was founded.
- **The Under**- The faerie realm. It's been divided into two parts ever since the Sidhe Queen and the Goblin king split up thousands of years ago. Mortals don't age in the Under, but it's a dangerous place for them to be. Getting lost means never being seen again, and it's easy to get indebted to

something nasty while trying to get through or out of the Under.

- **Wolf Messing Prep**- An institute for psychics to learn to control their skills before heading to college.

Events

- **The Big Reveal**- The term used for the 1990s, when the world discovered magic was real and extrahumans existed. The decade was marked with fear as everyone adjusted to the changes. Since the 21st Century, law and technology work for both humans and extrahumans.
- **Boston Internment**- A reaction by Boston government officials to the disappearance and suspected trafficking in extrahumans, especially shifters. All registered extrahumans in Boston lived on barges for close to a month under guard by the Boston Police. The traffickers got their hands on some magical gadgets, rendering the protection useless. Few survived.

THANK YOU!

Thank you for reading! If you loved this book, please leave a review. You can find my other work by clicking the links below, going to **my website** or visiting my **Author Central page**.

CONNECT WITH THE AUTHOR

Website: https://www.drperryauthor.com/

Join her newsletter!

Find more of D.R. Perry's books on Amazon.